POSIE'S CHRISTMAS PREDICAMENT

A Sugar Plum Romance

DARCI BALOGH

Knowhere Media

CHAPTER 1

Posie's first clue should have been the car.

Raised in New York City, she had ridden in the back of all types of vehicles; cars, buses, cabs, Ubers, even limos. But Posie Miller had never been in a Rolls Royce. Not in all of her thirty-some years on the planet.

Oblivious to its charms, she had barely given the luxury vehicle a second glance as she left the train station. Struggling with several bags – one for her clothes and two for her cake decorating tools – while searching through her pockets for her cell phone *and* adjusting to the bitter cold December air after being in a stuffy train for hours, Posie was preoccupied. When the extreme luxury car slid up next to her, she wasn't overly impressed.

"Miss Miller? Miss Posie Miller?" A big man wearing a crisp grey suit, matching wool coat, a black cap, and black leather gloves got out of the car and moved toward her on the platform. "Are you Posie Miller?"

She blinked up at him, her nose already freezing off of her face. What was it, minus 50 degrees? She should have wrapped her scarf around her whole head before stepping out of the train depot.

"Yes, I'm Posie Miller."

"I'm Thomas, the Reynolds' chauffeur. Please, allow me." Thomas picked up all of her bags like they weighed less than zero and showed her to the Rolls Royce.

Posie climbed into the back seat and Thomas closed the door. As she waited for him to deposit her bags into the trunk, she took in the plush leather seats and fine wood finishings. The car was smooth, elegant, warm – very warm, thank goodness. The Rolls was much more than Posie would have expected Georgina to send to pick up a lowly pastry chef, even if she had hired her specifically to wield her talents for the Reynolds' grand Christmas party.

Thomas slid behind the wheel. The window between the front seat and the back lowered.

He turned to look at her over his shoulder. "Are you comfortable?"

Sitting in the literal lap of luxury, Posie couldn't imagine not being comfortable. Physically at least. In truth, she had never had the kind of life that was filled with fine things and the Rolls Royce was causing a small fit of imposter syndrome.

"I'm fine, yes." She tried to smile with confidence. Glancing at all of the empty space in the back, she had a thought. "Are we picking up anyone else?"

"No, Miss Miller, just you."

"Please, call me Posie." She leaned back in the seat. "It's just this is so nice and roomy. I figured maybe we were going to pick up a couple of dignitaries...or some high up mafia boss."

Thomas looked at her in the rear view mirror. "No, no mafia bosses." He added with a chuckle, "Not today anyway."

She might have realized at that point that she was in over her head. That perhaps she wasn't completely prepared for what was to come. That her abilities were about to be tested to their limits and beyond. That she wasn't going to fit into the world she was entering.

But like many of life's most interesting adventures where one is blissfully unaware of what is about to unfold, Posie was lost in the minor details.

She knew she was only there for a week. And she knew she was expected to bake a cake, which she was well equipped to do. She swallowed the whispers of inadequacy that the Rolls Royce stirred up in her and tried to focus on those solid facts.

Of course, Georgina Andreanakis, now Mrs. R.C. Reynolds, was notoriously difficult to please and would expect something amazing, but Posie had no choice. The small bakery she had opened earlier in the year was floundering. No, more than that, it was sinking. About to go under. And she desperately needed this Christmas paycheck from one of New York's richest socialites to keep her head above water.

Turns out Posie was an excellent pastry chef, but a horrible business woman. She was at the point where she could barely afford to pay her assistant's meager salaries, let alone provide a decent living for herself. This big job creating a magnificent cake for Georgina's fancy-shmancy Christmas gala would pay Posie enough to buy some time. Fingers crossed, she could use that time to figure out how to run a bakery instead of merely knowing how to bake.

"How long will it take to get there?" Posie asked.

"Nearly two hours. The roads are a little hazardous in places. But we'll be fine. Help yourself to a drink." Thomas glanced up at her reflection in the rear view mirror again. "Do you have a music preference?"

Posie watched out the window as the Rolls Royce passed through a wintery landscape, heading away from the city and deep into the country to the Reynolds' famous estate, Long Point.

She shrugged. "How about some Christmas music? May as well get into the mood."

Tired from her trip, lulled into relaxation by the humming of the motor, and with nothing else to do, Posie dozed off to the sound of Michael Buble crooning Silver Bells. Meanwhile, the Rolls Royce whisked her off to a house and a family and a Christmas unlike any she had ever encountered before.

HER INITIAL OVERWHELM caused by the Rolls Royce was completely forgotten when they arrived at Long Point.

"Posie, are you awake? We're pulling into the drive now."

Thomas' voice floated into her sleeping brain. She was dreaming that she was trapped in a cave under a mountain of candy canes and the chauffeur's question brought her out of the dream right when the candy canes had started to tumble down on top of her head.

"Wha–?" She woke with a start, finding that she had slumped over so far she was practically laying down on the plush leather seat. She'd been sleeping so deep she had drooled. Posie used the sleeve of her coat to wipe the drool off the side of her mouth and the seat, but a dark spot remained on the leather. Drool didn't stain permanently, did it?

Sensing her panic, Thomas said, "You have about ten minutes until we get to the front door."

"Ten minutes?" She scooted forward and looked over the back of the front seat out the windshield. "To get down the driveway?"

Thomas didn't answer. There was no need. Once Posie

saw what lay in front of them she knew why it would take ten minutes.

They were on a private tree lined drive that stretched on and on into a dark landscape. All of the trees along the route were decorated with white lights. Every single one. This lit up the drive all the way to the house and she could see it was a long, long way.

"Wow," she muttered. Thomas merely chuckled again, a sound she was growing used to.

When they finally arrived at the house, or rather the mansion, the Christmas light decorations only amplified. All of the trees, shrubs, fences, statues and other outdoor structures glowed with white lights. The house had a story book look about it, made of stone with lots of interesting peaks. Every window was lined with white lights and hung with a glittering Christmas wreath. Not only that, the roofline and every architectural element was also lined with lights. Since the house was at least three stories high and a city block wide, the Christmas vibe was vigorous, to say the least.

Posie got out of the car and paused at the steps leading to the majestic front door. Two giant nutcracker statues guarded the bottom of the steps, which were wide enough to hold full sized Christmas trees – one on each side and on every step. The Christmas trees flanked anyone who dared climb up and face the giant dazzling wreath that was there to greet them on the door.

"Just. Wow." Posie stared.

Thomas joined her, carrying her bags. "It's something else, isn't it?"

"I almost need my sunglasses," she quipped.

Thomas smiled. "Are you ready to go in?"

Posie sighed. "As ready as I'll ever be."

Just before she followed Thomas onto the first step a flash of color caught her eye. She paused and looked harder, realizing there were an abundance of colorful Christmas lights to the far left of the mansion. It looked to be a different house or an outbuilding of some kind that was decorated in green and blues and reds instead of the bright white light of the main house. If they were actually in a story book, the smaller house with the colorful lights stood out so much Posie would guess it was an important character's house.

"Is everything all right?" Thomas had stopped climbing the steps and turned back to her.

"I'm just wondering who the renegade is that dared to use colored bulbs."

Thomas smiled and followed her gaze. "That would be the carriage house. Mr. Oliver tends to, how should I say, go against the flow here at Long Point."

Posie gave a mock sigh of disappointment. "There's always one, isn't there?"

"Indeed, there is, Miss," Thomas chuckled once more. "Shall we?" He motioned toward the blazing white wreath on the door.

"Lead on, Thomas, lead on." Posie turned away from the carriage house and hurried after the chauffeur to get inside out of the cold.

CHAPTER 2

Posie woke up early in the morning, bleary eyed. She hadn't slept well. Being in a new place didn't help, but she had also suffered from bad dreams all night. The most vivid had found her trying to make a batch of Christmas cookies to sell in her bakery, but a mean Scrooge type character from the bank kept sneaking up behind her and stealing huge handfuls of cookie dough, leaving her without enough left to make cookies.

"Doesn't take a genius to figure out that imagery," she muttered as she rummaged through her suitcase looking for her toothbrush.

She hadn't had time to unpack her things when the housekeeper, Margaret, finally showed her to her room the night before. Thomas had introduced her to Margaret and the butler, Bennet, when he deposited her and her luggage in the gigantic main entry hall before returning to the Rolls Royce.

"You'll meet the rest of the staff in the morning. We begin the day at 7:00am sharp, unless your duties require earlier hours," Margaret had informed her while eyeing Posie's less than Rolls Royce-y winter coat and hat. The housekeeper seemed a little pent up, in Posie's humble opinion, complete with greying hair pulled back into a tight bun. She had wondered briefly what Margaret would think about her own short hairdo, which was dyed a bright red, hiding underneath her hat.

"Eureka!" Posie pulled the small plastic bag holding her toothbrush and toothpaste out of her suitcase. Then, with much dismay, she noticed her wrinkled chef's pants and shirt. She should have hung them up when she got in. If she hung them up now, would they be presentable by 7:00 am? She glanced at the window. The sun was just coming up. "The real question is, what time is it?"

Posie hurriedly hung up her black pin striped slacks, her white chef's shirt with the big black buttons, and the crazy Christmas apron she had brought along for fun. Then, since her room wasn't equipped with a clock, she began a fresh hunt for her cell phone while brushing her teeth.

The frantic cell phone search was nothing new to her, as she had a bad habit of leaving phones in odd places. Today she was in an exceptional hurry. She wasn't used to being told when to show up for work. Technically she was on contract and didn't have to follow the same rules as an employee, but Posie really didn't want to end up on the bad side of sour faced Margaret. She needed to locate her phone and find out what time it was.

Her room was medium sized and nicely decorated in light blues. Equipped with a queen bed, a nightstand and lamp, a single dresser, a closet, and its own modest en suite, it didn't appear at first glance to be a vast area where a cell phone could slip into oblivion. But she had never met a space where she couldn't lose track of her cell phone, no matter how small.

As she passed the window, toothpaste building up in her

mouth, her nerves more and more on edge, she stopped suddenly, taken aback by the view.

Snow had blanketed the countryside over night, covering the buildings and gardens behind the house where Posie's window looked out. The grounds were immense and included a formal garden with hedges grown in geometric shapes, a large fountain in the center, and towering trees that had been formed into perfect cones.

In the distance, beyond the garden and past a swath of open space, was a long stable with paddocks along the side and a corral at one end. Past the stables were empty rolling fields and hills. The perfect place to ride.

A flicker of joy made Posie smile, which forced toothpaste foam out of her mouth. She hurried to the bathroom sink and finished brushing her teeth then returned to the window.

Several horses had come out into their paddocks. Two were beautiful bays with black manes and one was silvery white all over. Another one, a buckskin, with a shining pale brown body and black legs, tail and mane, was being led to the corral.

Posie sucked in her breath.

Her only memories of her parents taking her to the country when she was a kid was when they signed her up for horseback riding lessons. They had been an urban family, embracing everything about living in New York City, until her father had decided they needed to expand their horizons.

"She needs to know something about living outside the city," he had told her mother one morning before showing her an ad in the back of the newspaper offering discounted horseback riding lessons for children under 12. "This would be perfect."

In hindsight, it had been perfect. Eight weekends in a row they had driven into the country so Posie could learn how to ride. Right away she had loved the buckskin mare, Honey, and had been assigned to train on her for all of her lessons. By the end of the lessons Posie had learned to be comfortable around the large graceful horses and was a decent rider.

"We'll do this again next summer," her mother had reassured her when she broke down crying after her last lesson. "You'll see Honey then and can ride her again."

Of course, there hadn't been another summer with her parents after that one.

A familiar dull grief throbbed in Posie's heart as she watched the man lead the buckskin. Even still, she longed to find her way to the stables and be with the horses. Find out the name of this buckskin, stroke its muscled neck and pet its incredibly soft nose.

A muffled ringing interrupted her thoughts, bringing her back to her present predicament.

The ringing was definitely her cell phone. The muffled part was the problem.

"Where are you?" Posie whispered, waiting for the ring to come again, willing whoever was calling not to hang up.

It came again. From somewhere in her suitcase? She pulled all of her clothes out, tossing them unceremoniously on the floor. Nothing. The ring came again. From the wall? She pulled her suitcase away from the wall.

"There you are!" She snatched the phone off the floor where it must have slipped off of her suitcase when she opened it, saw who was calling and hit the answer button. "Hey, Bella!"

"Hi, you made it?" Bella had been her boss for a few years when she worked at her restaurant, Total, and her friend for longer than that. She was one of the few people in the world who kept up on Posie's every day activities, including checking in to make sure she got to her destination.

"Yes, I did. I was going to let you know last night when I got in, but it was late and then I couldn't find my phone."

Bella laughed. "Sounds like everything's normal then. How's Georgina?"

That was a loaded question. Bella knew all about Georgina and her temperamental ways after hosting her high society wedding at Total almost exactly three years ago.

"I haven't seen her yet. I did meet the housekeeper, and the butler, and the chauffeur. They picked me up in a Rolls Royce, can you believe that?"

Bella laughed again. "I can believe it. I wouldn't be surprised at anything you encounter there."

Posie fought back nerves. "That's true. I guess I'll see today."

"Just remember you're incredibly talented, Posie. Nobody could throw anything at you that you can't handle. Not even Georgina."

"Thanks, that reminds me, what time is it?"

"It's a quarter to seven. Sorry I called so early, I didn't know when you were going to head to the kitchen."

Her stomach tightened. "That's okay. I've got to go, though. I'm supposed to be downstairs at seven and I'm not even dressed yet!"

"All right, good luck. And remember, it's Christmas time, try to have some fun while you're there."

Bella's last piece of advice lingered in Posie's mind after she was dressed and checked her reflection in the mirror. The wrinkles had mellowed, sort of, and she looked presentable in her black and white pastry chef ensemble. Even with her bright red hair fixed into its jaunty spikes, the whole look lacked a certain festive sparkle.

Posie glanced at the crazy Christmas apron hanging on the doorknob of her bathroom. A full body apron, it was also bright red with giant green and blue ruffles on every edge. The front of the apron had a huge pocket, big enough to stuff with all kinds of goodies, and a big laughing Santa face next to a big laughing Cookie Monster face. Large bubble letters spelled out 'Christmas! Cookies!' to round out the look.

Posie twisted her mouth as she pondered her choices. Apron or no apron? Then, with a sigh of acceptance, she grabbed the apron off the bed. How could she *not* wear the Cookie Monster Santa apron? She put it on, looked in the mirror again and couldn't help but smile. The fact that Cookie Monster was wearing his own Santa hat took the apron to another level.

She cocked her head and gave her reflection a stern look. "It's Christmas, Posie, let's try to have some fun while you're here." Then she hurried out the door.

Fun was obviously not the name of the game with Margaret or the rest of the staff. She found them all lined up in the main hall, which was an imposing space. It connected the front door to the wide staircase and every other room on the main floor, but was large enough and beautiful enough it could have been a ball room all of its own.

Posie couldn't tell if Bennet the butler, the maids, and the personal chefs of the Reynolds family were normally pinched and uptight, or if they were just mirroring Margaret's attitude to keep their jobs, but there wasn't a joyful smile in the bunch. There were a lot of them, too. With only time to get a sweeping look at all of their faces before taking a spot at the end of the line, Posie would guess there were at least 25 staff members at full attention.

Given the grandeur of the room, tan and white checkered marble floors, crystal chandeliers, classic artwork, not to mention the towering Christmas tree decorated with plush red bows gracing the center of the hall, Posie knew her crazy Christmas apron stood out like a sore thumb. Still, a part of her was glad to be a beacon of fun amongst the dismal faces of the others.

"Thank you for finally joining us," Margaret said with an

air of disapproval at Posie's tardiness. It had been 7:03 when she checked her phone before walking into the hall.

Once again, Posie had to remind herself that she wasn't actually a member of this exacting woman's staff. She was a contractor, coming in as a specialty pastry chef at the behest of the owner of this house, the woman who paid this Margaret person's salary. Reminding Margaret of that fact may be something Posie needed to do during her stay at Long Point, but now probably wasn't the best time. Margaret didn't seem like the kind of woman one wanted to anger by openly confronting her in front of the whole staff.

"Happy to be here," Posie answered with the brightest smile she could muster. Surely her smile plus her apron could overpower any bitter old housekeeper's attitude.

Margaret offered a thin lipped smile of her own as her gaze flicked from Posie's punky hairdo down to the very merry Cookie Monster and Santa. With a barely perceptible wince, she switched her attention to Posie's still slightly wrinkly pin striped slacks.

"You are welcome to have the maids take your uniforms and other clothing to the laundry to be washed and...*pressed* properly while you're here."

Posie was a little impressed at how the woman could make a polite gesture and still have it sound like an insult. She smiled even brighter. "Thank you, that's very nice of you."

Bennet cleared his throat. "Let's get on with the schedule for today." Posie listened as Bennet started his instruction. He was easily the oldest person in the room by decades, which was saying something as Posie pegged Margaret to be somewhere in her 50's.

Bennet went on and on, reviewing the guests who were expected to arrive that day and the activities planned for them. The elderly butler clearly wasn't worried about upsetting Margaret, because he ignored any and all attempts she made at interjecting. He didn't seem to be bothered by anything, really. Possibly because he had lost some of his hearing.

She shifted on her feet. She wasn't really part of the daily tasks assigned to the staff. What she needed to do was find out when she could meet with Georgina and then check out the kitchen.

Just when she was trying to determine how to interrupt Bennet, Georgina's unmistakeable voice rang out from the top of the massive staircase and did the job for her.

"Posie! You're here, thank goodness!"

Bennet paused, looking up. Margaret and the others looked up as well as Georgina swept down the stairs, very much the grand mistress of her domain. Blonde tresses, perfect makeup, dressed in a sleek wool skirt and cashmere sweater, all in varying shades of taupe, and flashing fingers full of diamond encrusted rings, including her Flintstone sized diamond wedding ring, she was the picture of affluence.

"You made it!" Georgina walked straight up to Posie and gave her a socialite hug. Then she held her at arms length and looked down at her crazy apron, letting out a guffaw of laughter. "You're hilarious!"

Posie glanced at the rest of the staff who were watching her and Georgina's reunion with surprised interest. She wanted to explain that she had baked Georgina's wedding cake and had a particular relationship with their boss that lent itself to this personal greeting. Posie wished she could tell them that she had only joined their morning lineup because Margaret had insisted, she hadn't done it to show them up or as some kind of weird power move.

There was no way to convey any of that. Besides, Georgina had taken over the room.

"Have you had breakfast yet? I'm skipping it today. I've got a thousand things to do for the party. So many people are coming! Important people, if you know what I mean." Posie did not really know what she meant, but Georgina didn't seem to notice. "Anyway, I know we need to meet and go over what you'll be making. I've got some great ideas, by the way. But we'll have to do that tomorrow morning. In the meantime, I know you don't have any assistants with you and Rafael can't spare any of his." Georgina gave a quick nod to her head personal chef who was still standing in line. As they all were.

"Ma'am—" Margaret started to speak, but Georgina wasn't paying attention.

She gripped Posie's arm excitedly and moved aside, pushing a young woman holding Georgina's chihuahua, Koukla, in her arms. "This is my niece, Cleo."

If Posie had been charged with picking one person in that room who was related to Georgina, Cleo would have been her last choice. Nothing about the short, round, dark and dowdy young woman indicated she could be in the same bloodline as Georgina. She was so quiet and nondescript Posie hadn't even noticed her following Georgina until she put her front and center.

Georgina continued, "She loves all those baking shows. You know, like the English one? I can't remember the name of it. Anyway, she's here for the holiday and you need an assistant..." Georgina raised her eyebrows, waiting for Posie to fill in the blanks.

Professional politeness kept the smile on Posie's face even as a growing sense of dread kept her from answering.

Georgina laughed out loud at Posie's silence, which she perceived was meant as a joke. Oblivious to the look of terror on Cleo's pudgy face, she nudged her niece toward Posie and the other staff members. "Cleo's going to be your assistant! Isn't that a wonderful idea?"

CHAPTER 3

"You don't have to do this," Cleo said as she showed Posie the way to the kitchen.

The girl spoke so softly, Posie didn't understand. "Sorry, I couldn't hear you. What did you say?"

Cleo sighed. A pathetic snort of a sigh that added to her general demeanor of sloppy sadness. "I don't know anything about being in a kitchen or making fancy desserts. I just like watching that stuff on TV." She braved a pathetic glance at Posie. "You don't have to use me as your assistant if you don't want to. I won't tell my aunt."

Posie's natural empathy kicked in. "Well, everyone has to start somewhere. Do you really want to help or is your aunt pushing you to help?"

"Oh, I do want to help. I think it would be so much fun to make some of the things I see on TV," Cleo gushed.

"All right then, you can be my assistant. We'll start you off on the easy stuff so you can learn." The glow of happiness in Cleo's quiet eyes was enough for Posie to know she had made the right decision, even if having a newbie on board for a big job could sometimes be more hassle than not. "Though I can't promise we'll be making any of the crazy stuff you see on TV."

Cleo giggled. "Wait until you see the kitchen. I bet we could make anything in there."

Cleo was not wrong. The kitchen at Long Point was unlike any Posie had ever had the chance to bake in.

The room was a wide expanse of space with stone tiled floor and vaulted ceilings. There were fine cabinets painted a cool sage green with gleaming white quartz counter tops, almost like a kitchen in a normal home. But there were at least triple the amount of cabinets and countertops than a normal luxury kitchen, plus a giant island in the center with its own standard sized sink.

Posie counted four sinks total, four ranges, and six wall ovens. That didn't include the cream colored vintage style eight burner stove that was tucked into what must have been the original cooking fireplace of the old house. The ancient fireplace was built out of massive stones and was so big it could have been its own breakfast nook.

As fantastic as all of this was, there was something even more amazing to Posie. In what might have been the dining area of a standard kitchen, there was another large room built out and styled like a conservatory, with windows for walls and ceilings. In this area were several heavy wooden work tables with matching stools and a long dining table and chairs that could seat at least eighteen people comfortably.

"Isn't it beautiful?" Cleo asked.

The sight of the kitchen had stopped Posie in her tracks when she entered. Frozen in place, all she could do was gawk. She had never seen anything like it.

The kitchen at Long Point was a blend of a family kitchen, an industrial kitchen, and something more magical. Kind of like the kitchen she imagined Santa having at the

North Pole, complete with evergreen garland and plush red velvet bows that decorated the conservatory area.

"Hello, welcome!" Rafael, Georgina's head personal chef, waved at Posie and Cleo and hurried over, offering Posie a warm handshake and an even warmer smile. "Welcome, welcome, let me show you what we've set up for you. Would you like some coffee? A croissant?"

Posie's original thoughts about the staff turned out to be true. Without Margaret around, Rafael and his assistants, Althea and Rafael Jr., his son who everyone called Junior, were kind and fun loving. Of course, working in that kitchen would improve anyone's mood, Posie decided. She thought she could probably live her whole life without ever leaving that kitchen and die a happy person.

Posie munched on a fresh croissant and sipped a delicious cup of coffee as Rafael showed her what he had set aside as her working space in his kitchen. This included two work tables and an extra long folding table they had added on the most secluded section of the conservatory, the end of the island that had its own sink, two of the wall ovens, and several shelves inside the gourmet sized stainless steel refrigerator.

"Will this be enough room?" he asked. Before she could answer he remembered something else. "Wait, my apologies, there's more!"

There was, indeed, more. A walk in refrigerator, a walk in freezer, and a butler's pantry that was twice as big as Posie's kitchen in her apartment. Rafael and his crew had cleared spaces in all three for Posie to create her masterpiece.

"I think this will be plenty of space, thank you," Posie told him as Rafael, her, and Cleo leaned casually against the countertop in the butler's pantry and talked.

"You're very welcome. We're pleased to have you with us for the holiday. Never mind that we don't have to make the dessert ourselves," Rafael chuckled, crinkling up the crow's feet on the corners of his eyes.

Posie laughed. "I'm happy to be here and happy to make the dessert!"

"While you're here, there are probably a few things you will want to know," Rafael began, but was interrupted by Junior's head popping into the door of the butler pantry.

"She's here, Papa," Junior said, giving them all a wide eyed look of warning.

Rafael pushed away from the counter. "Tip number one, stay as far away from Margaret as you can." He looked at Cleo. "You can show her out?" Cleo nodded and Rafael left to deal with the head housekeeper on his own.

Relieved she was to be saved another encounter with Margaret, Posie was curious how they would escape. Wouldn't she see them when they left the butler's pantry?

"C'mon, you can bring your coffee," Cleo said as she inexplicably turned to face the back wall instead of the door.

Cleo placed her hand on the far right side of the solid wall and, suddenly, it wasn't so solid anymore. The wall was actually a door that opened and led them into a windowless hallway, lit only by wall sconces mounted every ten feet or so.

"This is the servant's hall. All of these big old homes have them." Cleo explained. She closed the butler pantry door and the air in the hallway got very quiet and heavy. She peered at Posie's face in the low light. "I know, it's a little creepy isn't it? They used to use candles or flashlights to move around in these, but it's a lot better since Oliver put up these lights."

"When was that?" Posie wondered how in the world anyone could have ever stood being in the dark hallway without the electric lights.

"About ten years ago. He built all of the lights himself."

Posie looked more closely at the ornate leaf design on the nearest wall sconce, trying to appreciate them while simultaneously wishing they would hurry up and get to wherever they were going so they could leave the cramped space.

"I was thinking, since you don't meet with Aunt Georgina until tomorrow, do you want to do something more fun today?"

"Sure, what did you have in mind?" Anything except stay inside the servant hallways.

Even without much light, Posie could see Cleo's face brighten. "Do you want to go to the stables with me?"

Several minutes later Posie was following Cleo to the stables. Wrapped in a borrowed wool jacket, complete with hat and gloves, that Cleo had grabbed from some hooks next to the secret servant back door into the gardens, Posie tromped through the fresh snow, trying not to let the coffee spill out of her mug.

"They haven't cleared the paths yet, are you okay?" Cleo glanced down at Posie's black sneakers, which were soaked from the wet snow, as were the bottoms of her pinstripe slacks.

"They're not exactly snow boots, but I'll be fine." Posie grinned. She didn't mind her feet getting a little cold if it meant she got to see the horses up close.

The stables were just as grand as the rest of the estate. Plus they were warm, not as warm as the house, but warmer than outside. The smell inside the stables took Posie back to her riding lessons. Hay, oats, straw, the leather of saddles and bridles, and the smell of the horses themselves all combined into a particular essence of the outdoors that made Posie smile.

"Cleo, what are you doing bringing coffee to the stables?" A booming male voice with an Irish accent came out of a nearby stall whose door was open.

Cleo reacted immediately to the voice. Her whole face

turned pink and she giggled girlishly. It didn't take long to realize why once the owner of the voice came out of the stall.

A well built man wearing olive green work pants and boots, a white shirt, red suspenders, and an olive green plaid cap pushed a wheelbarrow full of straw, letting it drop right in front of Posie and Cleo. His shirt was pushed up to the elbows and he wore a pair of worn work gloves, which only made the muscles on his forearms seem even more impressive. He had ink black hair and a short trimmed beard to match, which accentuated his square jaw. His eyes were sharp and twinkled with fun.

"Finn, how did you know we had coffee?" Cleo asked, a coy note in her voice that surprised Posie.

He gave her a stern look that even Posie knew was meant to tease. "Because I can smell it, that's how. And why would you be bringing coffee into the stables when you know I make the best coffee for miles around?"

Cleo giggled again then remembered that Posie was there, too. "Oh, Finn, this is Posie. She's a pastry chef."

"Where are my manners? I should have introduced myself." Finn tipped his hat at Posie. "Finn Wilder at your service, Miss." He looked back and forth between Posie and Cleo. "Are you fine young ladies here to ride this morning?"

Posie's fingers and toes tingled at the idea. She hadn't even considered the possibility that she could actually go for a ride. She glanced down at her soggy shoes and slacks. Definitely going to have to take up Margaret on her somewhat snarky offer of having her work clothes laundered.

"Oh, no, not today," Cleo answered for both of them.

A little crestfallen, Posie agreed, "Maybe another time."

"Of course, another time." Finn grinned, glancing down at her half empty and now totally cold cup of coffee. "How about a hot, fresh cup of Joe, then?"

Posie was about to agree, nothing sounded more pleasant

to her at the moment than sipping coffee with the handsome, amiable stable guy, when a different man's voice interrupted their conversation.

"Finn, have you got everything ready?"

All three of them turned in the direction of the voice to find a tall, somber looking man striding toward them. Finn's shoulders straightened and Posie knew without asking that the other man must be one of the Reynolds family.

"Yes, sir, I've got Honeycomb saddled for you."

Honeycomb? Posie wondered if the buckskin she had seen in the corral earlier had almost the same name as the buckskin she used to ride as a child.

"Good, thank you." The new arrival joined them, stopping next to Cleo.

He was younger than Posie had originally thought when she heard his voice. A little taller than Finn, but not quite as broad. He was dressed in more formal riding attire, including black leather gloves and hat, black wool riding pants and a fitted wool jacket.

He didn't look directly at Posie and she didn't know if she was offended or not. The fact that he wasn't watching her did give her a chance to take a good look at his face. It was a handsome face, maybe not as obviously masculine and hand-some as Finn's, but still pleasant enough.

Remembering her manners this time, Cleo spoke up, "Oliver this is Posie. She's the pastry chef Aunt Georgina got for the Christmas party."

Oliver looked up, locking his gaze onto Posie's. She lost her train of thought. The space between them seemed to sparkle like all of the little white lights decorating Long point and for one moment the stables, the horses, Cleo, and even Finn, fell away.

Oliver's eyes were deep emotional wells she felt like she could drop into and never find her way out. They didn't twinkle and flirt like Finn's, but they held her gaze so intensely she could not look away.

Posie was at once intrigued and unsettled. When Oliver finally broke the spell she was under by turning his attention to the far end of the stables, she realized she hadn't even registered what color his eyes were.

Without saying anything, Finn had ducked out of the conversation to fetch Honeycomb. Posie's heart warmed when she saw him leading the beautiful buckskin toward them, fully saddled and bridled. Finn stopped when he reached the three of them and Posie marveled at the size and splendor that was Honeycomb.

The horse was even more beautiful up close. Her shining coat was the exact shade of a forest deer and her luscious black mane was so thick and long it rippled when she shook her head. Posie had to remind herself not to reach out and stroke the horse's neck, even though she was lucky enough to be right next to her and longed to do so. It seemed too forward a move in the situation, to touch the horse that obviously belonged to Oliver.

Honeycomb shook her head again, prancing her front hooves a few times as she did. The metal in her bit and bridle jangled. Her shining black tail whipped back and forth. Posie had to bite her lips to keep from doing something silly like squeal or giggle. She felt like a young girl again while in the vicinity of this beautiful beast.

"The cold's made her a wee bit frisky this morning, Mr. Oliver." Finn gripped the reins firmly.

Oliver didn't respond, merely stepped forward and ran his leather gloved hand down the muscled neck of the horse, nodding. Posie watched as his magnetic gaze wandered over the head and neck of the beautiful Honeycomb. She could feel how much he loved the horse.

Finn glanced at Cleo then back to Oliver and cleared his

throat. "Your grandfather said he would be down this morning to ride. Will you be wanting to wait for him?"

Oliver stiffened, his hand still on Honeycomb's neck. The soft energy that had wrapped around the whole scene iced over. Honeycomb jerked her head back and stepped sideways, right into Posie. A thousand pounds of muscle hit Posie like a brick wall, knocking her off her feet.

She gasped, her arms flailing uselessly. Everything around her tilted and blurred. She was toppling over, headed toward the stable floor.

Then, abruptly, she wasn't.

Something – no, *someone* – had a tight grip on her and pulled her to her feet. Stunned, Posie looked at the black leather gloved hand holding her arm firmly, but gently.

She looked up into Oliver's eyes and found herself once again speechless.

"Careful," he said.

Posie blinked several times, heat threatening to rise in her cheeks and turn her beet red.

He let go of her arm just as abruptly as he had taken hold of it then bent over swiftly in front of her. Posie still hadn't caught her breath when he straightened back up with her hat, which must have fallen off in the tumble, in his hand.

Oliver brushed several bits of straw off of the borrowed wool cap and presented it to her. "Your hat," he said, his eyes lifting briefly to her bright red hair then back. This time with the smallest twinkle in them.

"Thank you," she managed to answer, though it came out a bit breathless, like a damsel in distress.

"No, Finn, I won't be waiting for my grandfather this morning." Oliver was speaking to Finn, but hadn't looked away from Posie yet. He paused, once again peering into her eyes. Entranced again, Posie couldn't look away.

A slow, quiet smile grew on Oliver's face. As she watched,

mesmerized, his expression turned his face into one of the handsomest she had ever seen.

Then, suddenly, with a quick touch of his fingers to the brim of his hat as a goodbye, he turned to Finn and took Honeycomb's reins. "Thank you, Finn, I'll take her out."

Without another word to any of them, Oliver led Honeycomb out into the snow covered yard outside the open stable doors. With one swift move he mounted the saddle. Honeycomb pranced with all four hooves, excited to go on the ride.

Before they took off, Oliver turned the frisky horse in a circle so he could look once more into the stables. Posie couldn't really tell at that distance if he was looking directly at her, but she felt his eyes on her regardless.

Then they were gone. The sound of hooves clattered on old stone then muffled when they reached the end of the yard.

Posie stared at the empty space where they had just been, her heart pounding in her chest. Why did she feel like she was in the middle of a Jane Austen movie?

CHAPTER 4

In the wee hours of the morning on her second day at Long Point, Posie was once again hunting frantically through her room for her cell phone.

"No, no, no, no..." she muttered as she dumped her suitcase out onto the unmade bed. Nothing.

It was still early, extremely early, but she had woken up with a start when her sleeping brain remembered she hadn't plugged in her cell the night before.

The whole day had been a whirlwind of activity. After her tour of the stables, and the rest of the immense mansion, she had spent several hours unpacking her decorating tools and getting everything she would need set up in the kitchen to start baking after her meeting with Georgina.

She had eaten both lunch and dinner with the staff at the long dining table in the conservatory. After dinner she had gathered together all of her clothes, minus her pajamas, to give to Isla, the maid who had volunteered at dinner to have her things laundered and pressed and returned to her first thing in the morning.

By the time Posie showered and went to bed she was

exhausted and hadn't had a second thought about her cell phone, until the fear of its loss woke her up long before sunrise.

She had been searching for it ever since. Sleepy and annoyed, she cursed her forgetfulness as she pored over every inch of the bathroom and bedroom, hunting through drawers and behind furniture. Her hapless quest culminated with the final dump of the contents of her suitcase.

Posie threw her hands up in the air. In the quiet of pre-dawn, she whisper yelled into the empty room, "I need to know what time it is!"

Flopping onto the bed she retraced her steps from the day before. The last time she had used her phone was when she spoke to Bella first thing in the morning. She had a distinct memory of putting it in her pant's pocket before donning the Santa Claus Cookie Monster apron.

After that, she couldn't remember using it at all. But there was no reason it should have fallen out of her pocket during the day. Her pinstripe chef slacks had deep pockets. And she hadn't done anything overtly physical that might have caused it to—

"Except!" Posie sat straight up.

She had been jostled around and almost fell when Honey-comb bumped into her. And she'd been pretty distracted by Oliver grabbing her arm. It was possible her phone could have popped out of her pocket and dropped to the ground unnoticed. Especially if it fell into straw or hay, which would have muffled any noise it might make when it hit the floor.

She scrambled off the bed and hurried to the window. It was still dark outside, only the faintest of grey of the coming dawn tinted the black night. The only visible sign of the stables was a single yard light shining in the distance.

Posie could get there, find her phone, and be back before the sun even came up. No problem.

Turning back to the bed she stopped short.

"Ugh! My clothes!" Posie covered her face with her hands and groaned. Dropping her hands she glared down at her flannel pajamas and shook her head in disgust. Every piece of clothing she had brought was still with the maid.

She shook her head with a jerk and made a decision. Catching her reflection in the mirror she gave herself a hard look. "You know what? I don't care. You need your phone to be on time *and* to actually have the meeting with Georgina. All of the pictures of cake examples are on it."

Several minutes later Posie was making her way through the dark, snow covered gardens. Wearing her bright blue flannel snowman pajama pants and shirt, her own jacket and hat, and a pair of heavy boots she had borrowed from the servant's entrance at the back door, she was protected from the bitter cold, but still muttering crossly to herself about the whole situation.

At the edge of the formal gardens was a strip of wild landscaping. A large grove of trees blended into tall grasses and shrubbery that weren't sculpted like the lawns, though there was a rough path leading through them.

Posie didn't remember it being a very long walk from the gardens through the wild area to get to the stables when she had gone with Cleo. However, Cleo had been there to guide her – and it had been daylight.

In the stinging cold of dark morning air, the path through the wild area seemed to stretch on and on and on. As she trudged for what felt like thirty minutes her resolve started to fall apart. Maybe she should have thought through this little outing before taking off all by herself.

Posie stopped walking. The light from the stables blinked at her through the black trunks of several barren trees in the near distance. She turned back toward the back of the main house. Most of the windows were still dark, yet there was plenty of light spilling out over the snow from the lamps that shone at both visible doorways.

Still, she was now closer to the stables than the main house. It would be a shame to come all this way and turn around without getting her phone. Besides, she didn't want it to get accidentally stepped on by a passing horse. All she needed was the extra expense of buying a new cell phone.

Her mind made up, Posie turned back to the stable and started walking. Faster now as the light of morning didn't appear to be making a dent in the pressing darkness of the wild area.

She arrived at the barren trees, emerging on the other side of them feeling accomplished and looking forward to getting inside of the warm stables. She would find her phone and, hopefully, dawn would break before she headed back to the main house, offering light for her return walk.

Smiling at what she thought was a pretty well laid out plan for so early in the morning, Posie pushed through the last bit of heavier snow that had built up on the edge of the wild path and into a well lit yard. There, she stopped short and stared up at a building that was not the stables. Not even close.

It was a house. Built in the same style as the main house, but not as monumental. Striking in its own way, however, with similar architectural features as the main house and set inside of a private garden, Posie thought it was one of the prettiest houses she had ever seen.

But it being a house meant someone lived there, which meant she was trespassing.

Glancing around to see if she could figure out where she had gone wrong in her attempt to get to the stables, Posie decided to step back into the darkness of the wild area. No reason to alarm anyone inside by her presence, if they were even awake at this hour of the morning.

That's when she heard it.

A low guttural sound coming from somewhere inside the dark grove of barren trees.

Posie froze. The hair on the back of her neck stood up underneath her heavy wool coat.

Up until that moment, the silence of the estate grounds had made her a little uncomfortable. She was used to the bustle of New York City after all. But the quiet that fell over her now was different – ominous.

Her heart thudded in her chest. The sound of her own breathing was too loud. She wished she could silence it, keep quiet and hide from...what, exactly?

Her rapidly panicky breath made plumes of frosty air in front of her face as she peered into the dark. Had she been imagining things? Making something out of nothing, like she tended to do when she was out of her element?

Nope.

There it was again. Louder this time.

No longer an unfamiliar low sound that she couldn't put her finger on. Posie knew exactly what was coming out of the unlit wildness – the growling of a dog.

A big dog.

And not just one.

The deep belly growling came out of the dark from two distinct, separate, places.

Posie sucked in her breath, willing herself not to make a peep. Something told her if she made any kind of noise or moved suddenly the dogs would attack.

Her mind clicked quickly through her options. Stand still and hope they lost interest. Not a reliable outcome in her opinion. Go back up the path to return to the main house? Oh, heck no.

The only plan she could come up with was to inch her way backwards toward the silent house, knock on the door, and hope somebody would let her in before she got her throat ripped out.

She took the tiniest step back, keeping her eyes on the dark trees where the vicious sounds were emanating from. Nobody had warned her there were dangerous animals lurking around on the property. Of course, they probably hadn't imagined the guest pastry chef would be wandering around the grounds in the middle of the night.

If only the sun would come up. Although then Posie might be able to see her attackers. She wasn't sure that would make her feel better.

After what might have been a few minutes, which felt like hours, of taking tiny, slow, careful steps backwards, Posie braved a glance over her shoulder to see how far she had come.

Not far at all. The space between her and the safety of the house seemed to have stretched into a football field length since she had originally arrived. And the growling had not ceased for one moment.

Her stomach dropped. She didn't know how long dogs normally growled before they attacked, but she didn't like her odds.

Suddenly, a light switched on in the front window. A startled squeak escaped Posie's throat.

That was enough to trigger the beasts waiting in the trees. Their growling seethed into snarls and vicious barks. Even before she had spun around to face them Posie knew they were running straight at her to attack.

She screamed.

A door crashed open.

A man shouted.

All of Posie's attention zeroed in on two German Shepherds racing toward her, hackles sticking straight up, sharp teeth snapping. She stumbled back, tripping over her own feet while trying to get away.

More lights came on. Colored Christmas bulbs spilled bright cheery light all over the yard and house. The irony of being mauled to death amidst the decorative lights of Christmas did not escape her, but she had no time to process it. There was another sound. A growl so deep and menacing it must be coming from a bear. Was a bear about to attack her from behind?

She couldn't fight off two German Shepherds at the front and defend against a bear assault from behind at the same time. With nowhere to go, she let out a shriek of terror, threw both of her arms up to protect her head and dropped to the snowy ground in a tight ball.

The bear jumped right over her.

Her eyes squeezed shut in fear, Posie heard rather than saw what happened next. Snarls and scuffles, vicious barks raising in pitch to something more like yelps. A man shouting from somewhere nearby. More deep growls and even deeper barks. Then silence. The battle was over.

Posie couldn't move. Her hands and arms trembled, but remained clutching her head. Tremors moved through her stomach and she let out a small whimper.

More scuffling came right beside her then a hand touched her back.

"Are you all right?" The man again. Right next to her now. Before she could answer, a huge wet tongue stuck through a space between her arms and shoved itself directly into her ear. The man scolded, "Hagrid, get back!"

Posie jerked away from the tongue. But the sensation had helped bring her back to her senses. She let her arms drop and opened her eyes, getting her first look at who had saved her from the German Shepherds.

CHAPTER 5

Oliver stood over her, wearing nothing but a pair of blue striped pajama pants, a navy blue robe, which hung open because he hadn't had time to tie it, a pair of slippers, and a harsh glint in his eyes.

Next to him was the animal she presumed to be responsible for running off the German Shepherds. Not a bear, but a dog the size of a bear. If he hadn't been pure black she would have assumed he was a St. Bernard. Whatever he was, he sat obediently still and panted at her with happy anticipation.

"What are you doing out here?" Despite Oliver's obvious irritation, he reached down and offered her his hand.

Too weak to get up on her own, Posie took it and allowed him to help her into a standing position. Her hat had fallen off in the mayhem. Oliver bent down and picked it up, knocking the snow off and handing it to her while eyeing the bottom of her pajama pants, which had come untucked from her borrowed boots during the kerfuffle.

She put her hat on with shaking hands and looked Oliver straight in the eye, purposefully ignoring the section of his bare muscled chest revealed by his open robe. Posie hoped to project an image of someone who had not been in a fetal position on the ground screaming in terror only a few moments before.

"I was looking for my cell phone." These weren't the words she thought were going to come out of her mouth, but she wasn't completely in control of her faculties at the moment.

Oliver let out a quick, scornful snort. "Cell phone?" He looked around their surroundings in a sarcastic show of searching for her phone and frowned. "Why would your cell phone be here?"

She shook her head and concentrated on choosing the right words. "I got lost. I was trying to go to the stables."

He glanced into the grove of barren trees. "It can be a dangerous thing, roaming around these grounds at night."

"I see that now." Posie swallowed back tears that were pushing at the back of her throat. "Thank you...for helping me."

Oliver looked into her eyes, the same way he had when they first met in the stables, as if he was searching for something. Posie couldn't look away. Her tears subsided, but she started to shiver.

"That was Hagrid. Not me. He doesn't put up with those so-called guard dogs." At the mention of his name Hagrid stood and wagged his tail, watching Oliver expectantly. Oliver looked down into his giant dog's eager face and his expression softened. He sighed and jerked his head toward Posie. "Go on, say hello."

In one great bound Hagrid was in front of her. Posie flinched, still in fight or flight mode. The huge dog seemed to sense her fear and lowered to his belly, resting his great head on his front paws and giving her literal puppy dog eyes.

"Thank you, Hagrid." Posie reached down and pet the top of his head with fingers that still trembled. To further show

how safe she was, Hagrid immediately rolled onto his back, exposing a massive chest and belly she was invited to rub.

"All right, that's enough." Oliver commanded. Hagrid jumped up, shook the snow out of his thick black fur, and trotted toward the house. Oliver pulled his robe closed and tied it as he peered at her. "You're cold. Come inside."

Flustered, Posie tried to decline gracefully. "Please, I don't want to bother you. Can you just tell me how I get to the stables from here?"

Oliver coughed out a laugh. "You're not going back out there with the dogs on patrol. They'll be locked up at seven. Come in." It wasn't really an invitation, more along the lines of a command, and Oliver didn't wait for an answer. He turned away from her and started up the path to the front door.

She glanced around at the morning that continued to stay dark as night and argued meekly, "But...I need my phone for my meeting...and to tell the time."

Oliver stopped short. He looked over his shoulder at her and scoffed. "You do not need a cell phone to tell time." With a shake of his head he continued up the front steps and said, without looking back, "Come in out of the cold."

Walking into Oliver's carriage house was like going back in time. High ceilings, great arched doorways, solid wood plank flooring that had been finished to a gleaming shine, and what looked like original iron hardware on the doors and windows.

But what really carried Posie into a different time and place were the clocks.

Every square inch of available space held a clock. And not just regular clocks, either. Beautiful, ornately carved, antique clocks sat on the fireplace mantle, coffee table, and hung on the walls. They shared space with lamps on the side tables and books on several floor to ceiling bookshelves.

From the instant she walked through the door, the mellow sound of coordinated ticking filled the space. The sight of all of the clocks, including not one, but two, fantastic grandfather specimens, took Posie's breath away for a few moments.

"I'll fix some coffee," Oliver announced as he disappeared down the hallway. "You can leave your hat and coat on the rack."

Posie did as he requested, all the while admiring the elegant coat rack and the tan and white checkered design of the marble entryway floor. Glancing down at her snowy boots, she decided to remove them as well. It didn't seem right to make a mess on his floors after Oliver, and Hagrid, quite possibly had saved her life.

In her stocking feet she moved quietly into the living room, admiring each of the individual clocks as she went and marveling at the collection as a whole. There were clocks of all shapes and sizes, unlike any she had ever seen before. There was even one that served as the bottom of a decorative birdcage hanging from its own stand and hook.

The whole room felt a little like a mad inventor lived there, but with Christmas overtones. Like the mad inventor also made specialty toys for Santa Claus.

Besides an overstuffed couch and reading chair, there was an unlit Christmas tree in the corner of the living room between the fireplace and the front window. One big red stocking with the letter H embroidered on the front hung from the mantle. In the opposite corner was a large drawing table covered with unruly stacks of paper, and more. The small lamp on the drawing table was the only light on in the room and it illuminated all manner of small tools, magnifying glasses, wires, wheels, and what appeared to be the innards of a clock.

As Posie perused the unusual decor of Oliver's living room, one particular clock on the mantelpiece caught her eye. Encased in a glass globe it, too, had an air of Christmas. A Charles Dickens style Christmas.

Inside the globe was an old fashioned horse and sleigh made out of gold. Not solid gold, but rather thin sheets of the stuff that had been meticulously constructed. The face of the clock was built into the side of the sleigh and as each second clicked by the legs of the horse switched back and forth, giving it the appearance of movement.

A click sounded in the entryway and the Christmas tree lights came on, revealing that not only the tree was decorated, but the mantle itself and a huge wreath hanging above it. The twinkling colors transformed the already remarkable room into something even more magical.

Posie whirled around to find Oliver leaning against the doorway watching her, Hagrid at his side. He, too, was in his stocking feet. But now he also wore black framed glasses and had changed into jeans and a heavy cable knit sweater. How long had she been prowling through the living room?

She looked hurriedly around, searching for an explanation as to why she had been blatantly invading his privacy. Finding none, she simply said, "It's beautiful."

The sides of his mouth tugged up into an almost smile, then he pushed off the wall and turned back down the hallway. "Coffee's ready."

Hagrid remained, cocking his big furry head at her until she moved to follow his master. The dog followed her down the hallway, escorting her to the kitchen.

Two mugs of hot coffee sat on an island at the center of a charming kitchen that had been built at the end of a peaked roof, so the beamed ceiling slanted upward. The cabinets were well made, painted deep green, and made the whole space warm and inviting. The coffee helped with that, too.

"Do you take cream and sugar?" Oliver's head was stuck inside the refrigerator when she and Hagrid entered.

"Cream, please." Posie settled onto one of the stools next to the island and took the pint container of cream from Oliver when he handed it to her.

Oliver spooned sugar from a sterling silver sugar bowl into his cup. "Thor and Diesel belong to my grandfather."

"Who?" Posie took a sip of the hot coffee. Delicious.

"The German Shepherds. They're his guard dogs and they're vicious. They should be put down." Oliver glanced up when Posie made a sympathetic sound. "Or at least locked up."

Posie stroked the top of Hagrid's head, thinking about how different he and the terrifying German Shepherds were.

Oliver added cream to his coffee then put the container back in the refrigerator. "They're nothing but a damned menace. He hasn't trained them properly, only taught them to be mean."

Feeling more forgiving now that she was safe and had something warm to drink, Posie offered, "Isn't that what guard dogs are supposed to do, though? I mean, I was a stranger and I was walking around where I wasn't supposed to be."

Oliver lifted one eyebrow and looked at her skeptically. "You're awfully tolerant."

Posie shrugged. "I'm just thankful you, um....and Hagrid were there to help me."

Hagrid's tail thumped on the floor when she said his name. Posie smiled and ruffled the fur behind his flopping ears.

"Now you're just flattering him." Oliver took his coffee to the table where a pair of boots waited on the floor next to his chair.

Posie watched as he put on the boots and started lacing them up. "Busy morning ahead?"

Oliver didn't look up. "I'm taking you to the stables."

Posie flushed with embarrassment. "Oh, no, you don't have to do that. I don't want to bother you."

He raised his eyes to hers as he continued tying his laces. He didn't need to say what he was thinking, she could read it all over his face. She had already bothered him. What was one more inconvenience now that he was in this deep?

"I can't guarantee the dogs won't be back around so you can't go alone." Finished, Oliver stood up and took a big slug of his coffee. When she didn't answer, he studied her face more carefully and seemed to understand that she was feeling guilty. "It's not a bother. Besides, Hagrid will be glad for the early morning walk, won't you boy?"

In answer to that question, Hagrid let out one booming woof and ran to the front door.

As they walked, dawn finally kissed the dark sky, turning it a soft grey and allowing Posie to see across the landscape and realize how far off course she had gotten on her way to the stables. She must have taken the completely wrong path out of the formal gardens to arrive on Oliver's doorstep.

It was still freezing cold, but walking kept them warm. Hagrid didn't mind the temperature. He bounded around them in big circles then took off full speed running and woofing into the distance only to return and bound around them again.

Their breath showed in great puffs in front of their faces as they walked and talked. When Oliver turned to look at her, Posie could see that his glasses had fogged up.

"Why is it that you so desperately need your cell phone at this ungodly hour?"

Posie sighed. "Well, first of all, there isn't a clock in my room." She eyed him, wondering if he, too, found that a little funny. He did. An actual grin was on his face and his eyes held the hint of laughter. She continued, "So I need it for my alarm. I need to be on time. But also it has all of my pictures to reference for the cake I'm making for...Mrs. Reynolds."

"Ah, that's right. You're making my new Aunt Georgina's grand dessert."

"Correct. That's the whole reason I'm here."

"Fair enough." Oliver resigned himself to their task of retrieving her cell phone, but not without shaking his head and adding, "I'm not a fan of the things."

"Desserts or cell phones?"

He smiled, a real smile. "Cell phones."

"No?"

He shook his head and watched as Hagrid plowed through a snow drift in the distance at full speed. "I've always been more comfortable with things I can actually take apart and fix if I need to."

Posie nodded, she already knew that about him from being inside of his house.

When they arrived at the stables, Finn was there. He rounded the corner and started at the sight of them.

"Good morning, sir." He glanced quickly at Posie and tipped his hat, expertly ignoring her snowman pajama pants. "Are you here to ride?"

Oliver stiffened and answered in a voice too loud for the circumstances, "No, Finn, we're here to retrieve Miss Posie's cell phone."

Posie couldn't help but look at Oliver. His whole demeanor had changed the instant Finn appeared. She didn't know a person could come across as both austere and awkward, but Oliver was pulling it off.

At the same time, hearing him say her name stirred a pleasant feeling in her chest. She liked the idea that they were on this odd early morning quest together and she found it a compliment that he had remembered her name.

There was an embarrassing pause as Finn seemed to take

in their situation and, most likely, make assumptions. Posie had to suppress a smile as Oliver grew more and more ruffled.

Finally, Finn turned his full attention onto Posie, a flash of amusement in his handsome eyes. "I can fetch your phone for you. Give me a quick minute to take a look."

"Oh, no need, thank you. I'm pretty sure I know where it is." Posie hurried toward the stable doors. Oliver and Hagrid followed.

Sure enough, her phone was exactly where she had almost fell after being bumped by Honeycomb. On the ground, next to the wall, hiding in the shadows. Posie picked it up and inspected it for cracks.

"All's well, then?" Oliver asked, leaning over her shoulder to see.

"It doesn't look like a horse has stepped on it or anything. But it's freezing cold and it's dead." She sighed. "So I still won't know what time it is."

Oliver chuckled. The sound so close to her ear sent a pleasant sensation through her body.

"I can help you with that," he said, digging into the inside chest pocket of his wool coat and pulling out a pocket watch. He flipped it open and Posie could see the gleam of silver. She had no doubt the watch was old and guessed it was worth more than she made in a month.

Before Oliver could give her the time, a loud whinny came from a nearby stall and Honeycomb stuck her head out to see what they were up to.

"Honeycomb!" Posie couldn't contain her excitement at seeing the beautiful horse.

Oliver snapped his eyes to hers, perhaps surprised she remembered the horse's name. Posie moved carefully up to Honeycomb and gently stroked her soft nose. The horse breathed out gusts of warm air onto her hand.

Oliver watched her curiously. "Do you ride?"

Posie shrugged, completely enrapt with Honeycomb. "I had lessons when I was a kid, but I haven't ridden in a long time."

Hagrid approached the stall wagging his great tail lazily. He stuck his nose up toward the horse and Honeycomb lowered her head to smell him in greeting. Hagrid's big wet tongue stuck out and licked the horse's nose. Honeycomb threw her head back and tossed her mane, making Posie laugh.

"Would you like to?" Oliver asked.

Posie turned to face him where he was leaning casually against the heavy post at the corner of Honeycomb's stall. "Would I like to what?"

He grinned. "Go for a ride."

Her eyes flew open. "Really?"

He nodded. There was a flirty sparkle in his eyes, which made it difficult for Posie to think straight. Visions of riding on top of Honeycomb as she galloped across an open field with Oliver riding next to her raced through her mind. Despite wishing she could remain poised, a joyful smile spread across Posie's face. She had to look away to hide what seemed like a wild overreaction to his offer.

Her eyes fell on the rays of morning sunshine streaming through the open stable doors behind him. A few brave birds sang their greetings to the cold morning. With a sudden gasp, Posie's mind snapped back to reality.

She shot a panicked look at Oliver. "What time did you say it was?"

CHAPTER 6

Georgina requested to have their meeting in the grand ballroom where Posie's cake would be on display for the Christmas gala.

"As long as there's a plug for my charger," Posie said to herself as she returned Georgina's text with a *Sounds good* and a thumbs up emoji.

She had taken a quick shower after racing back from the stables, on the correct path this time, and her phone was almost thawed out. It was only at 2% power, however, and she was supposed to be at the meeting in 15 minutes. It would need to charge while she showed Georgina all of the images of cakes she wanted to use as inspiration for her Christmas creation.

Thank goodness Isla had come through. When Posie arrived back at her room she found all of her clothes cleaned, neatly pressed, and put away. She blew her hair dry as quickly as possible, threw on her pinstriped slacks and chef shirt and decided against the Santa Cookie Monster apron for now. It didn't seem to fit with the idea of meeting in a ballroom.

As she entered the grand ballroom, a room Cleo had left

off of her tour, Posie was glad she didn't have any cartoons emblazoned across her chest. When Georgina had called it the grand ballroom she had not been kidding.

Dark wood walls stretched into cathedral style ceilings. Not the kind of cathedral ceilings that were found in someone's home, but the kind of cathedral ceilings that were found in enormous ancient churches. There were wide cathedral arched entryways on opposite ends of the ballroom and the design was repeated in tall windows along one side of the room as well as enclaves that were built into the walls along the other three sides.

Eight massive chandeliers hung in two rows of four, pouring light across a smooth marble floor that had the same pattern of tan and white checkers repeated from the main hall and Oliver's house, but these checkers were gigantic in comparison. Several elegant banquet tables had been placed against one wall in between the enclaves, which each held a sparkling Christmas tree.

The decorations didn't stop there. Pine garland with red bows draped across the top of every window, which also held matching pine wreaths. More wreaths graced the wall spaces between the enclaves, but the main attraction in the grand ballroom had to be the giant Christmas tree in the center of the floor.

Posie had to remind herself not to gape like a five-year old as she walked past the tree. It had to be at least 40 feet tall, maybe even more. The largest tree she had ever seen was the tree at Rockefeller Center and this one was just as impressive because it was indoors. Standing next to it, she felt like a child again.

"Yoo-hoo, Posie, we're over here!" Georgina called out from the far corner of the ballroom where she and Cleo were sitting at one of the banquet tables.

"This is really beautiful," Posie gushed when she joined them.

Georgina smiled, fully aware of the majesty she had gained access to when she married R.C. Reynolds. She patted her hand on the empty chair next to her. "It's going to be even more amazing when we get your fantastic creation in here for the party."

"Yes! Great..." Posie looked around for an outlet nearby.

"Now, I'm thinking of something really different. Something that will just blow people away." Georgina spread her fingers out and made jazz hands to indicate exactly how blown away people should be when they saw Posie's cake.

"Of course, I've been thinking about it a lot. I have some example cakes to show you on my cell." Holding her charger in one hand, Posie ducked to look under the table, checking for any possible outlets hidden there.

Georgina laughed with delight. "But that's the thing. I don't want a cake!"

Posie straightened up and stared at her client. Georgina was clapping her hands together gleefully.

The repercussions of missing out on this Christmas payday smashed through Posie's mind, knocking out every other thought. Not making payroll in January for her bakery employees. Not having any money to pay herself, which meant she wouldn't make rent on her apartment in February. Come to think of it, without Georgina's big check she wouldn't be able to pay rent on the bakery either.

Posie swallowed. Hard. "You don't want a cake?"

"No! I have an idea for something even better. And I just know you're the one to bake it!" Georgina's loud laugh and wide smile relayed how unaware she was that she had almost given her guest pastry chef a mild heart attack.

Posie sat slowly down in a chair, shoving her now unnecessary phone charger into her pocket along with her cell phone. "What do you have in mind?"

Georgina swept her arm down the banquet table. "All of this space is set aside for it."

The table was long. About 18-feet was Posie's guess. What kind of dessert would take up all of that room?

Answering her unspoken question, Georgina announced, "Gingerbread!"

"Gingerbread?" Posie found herself once again staring at Georgina, unable to respond.

Georgina nodded with such exuberance her long, blonde, thoroughly straightened hair rippled. She touched Cleo on the shoulder, who had remained sitting quietly beside her aunt through the whole conversation, holding the ever present Chihuahua in her lap.

"It was Cleo's idea," Georgina said.

Cleo's eyes widened. "I, uh...it was?"

"Yes, you silly," Georgina's laughter echoed through the huge ballroom. "Remember? You showed me that picture of the gingerbread city?"

Cleo obviously didn't remember. Posie didn't care. It didn't matter where the idea came from, the only thing that mattered was she was going to have to start from scratch. All of her designs had been for an elaborate cake, which was a far cry from an elaborate gingerbread house.

Posie winced, one word that Georgina had said stood out in her mind. "Did you say gingerbread *city*?"

"Yes! Isn't a marvelous idea? This whole table full of a hustling, bustling beautiful gingerbread city!" Georgina made more grand sweeping gestures with her arms, thrilling at what she saw in her mind's eye.

Posie took in the 18-foot long banquet table. Gingerbread city. That was a lot of cookie buildings. She would need to plan out the structures so they were different heights and build them well enough that they wouldn't collapse.

A sharp memory of the last gingerbread house she had built entered her mind. It had been gorgeous, but didn't last very long. She hadn't baked the gingerbread long enough and the walls had caved in under the weight of the frosting and candy decorations. She winced again at the memory. That gingerbread house had only been for fun to decorate her own house, not for a client.

Georgina stood up and went to the end of the banquet table, studying it with a comically thoughtful expression. "Do you think this will be enough room? We could dedicate another table to it."

"No!" Posie stopped her. "I mean, yes, it's enough room. We won't need any more." She wasn't sure she would be able to fill up the already designated space. Ideas started clicking through her mind. She would have to get busy creating the designs if she wanted to get everything baked, cooled, and assembled before the Christmas party. Thinking out loud, she said, "I'm going to need *a lot* of cookie sheets."

"Of course, whatever you need," Georgina answered. "Just tell Rafael, he can get any supplies we don't already have." She beamed at Cleo then Posie. "And Cleo will be at your side, too. Don't forget."

Posie gave her a weak smile. "Right, I haven't forgotten."

Footsteps sounded as two well dressed men entered the ballroom. One Posie recognized as R.C. Reynolds, Georgina's husband. He was a handsome man who moved with the confidence of wealth and power. Posie didn't know the other man, who was older than R.C. and the better dressed of the two. He had the same level of confidence as R.C., even more, but he also had a severe crease in his brow that gave him a more intimidating vibe.

"Darling!" Georgina exclaimed, moving smoothly across

the marble floor to greet her husband. "We're just going over some things for the party."

R.C. gave Georgina a light kiss on the cheek. "Good, I'm sure it will be beautiful." He gave Posie a polite smile. "Posie, it's nice to see you again."

Posie plastered on her best professional cake baker smile. "Thank you, it's nice to see you as well."

R.C. touched Georgina's arm. "My lovely wife is much happier knowing you're in charge of the dessert."

"Oh? That's so nice of you to say." Posie felt a little sick.

"I hear it's going to be a real showstopper," he continued.

"You don't even know, darling. It's going to be the talk of the season!"

The older gentleman scowled, apparently not interested in whether or not a cake – or cookie – would be the talk of anything. Posie couldn't blame him. She, too, was having difficulty making small talk as the weight of what she had to do to bake and build this masterpiece continued stacking up in her mind.

Georgina ignored the older man. "You should see the guest list! Not only is this party going to be the biggest Christmas event this year, possibly of any year, ever, but it's also our anniversary, don't forget."

"How could we forget, Georgina, when you will not stop talking about it," the older man spat the words at Georgina so viciously the air in the ballroom turned instantly heavy and sank to the floor. Nobody could breathe.

Georgina paled. Posie had never seen her look so stunned, but Posie had never seen anyone rebuke the socialite either.

"Father–" R.C. started, but the old man wasn't hearing any of it.

"What, Randolph? Would you have us stand here all morning and twiddle away our day discussing cheese dip and cupcakes?" He threw his arm in Posie's direction, jabbing his finger at her as if she herself was an undesirable snack food.

"Father, please, not now." R.C. meant not in front of the help, but Posie didn't get the feeling his father was going to pay him any mind.

The elder Mr. Reynolds opened his mouth to speak, but Posie beat him to it.

"Excuse me, Mr. Reynolds, Mrs. Reynolds." Posie nodded courteously, nearly curtsied, at Georgina and R.C. in turn in an attempt to show them the utmost respect. More respect than she showed R.C.'s father. "I love the changes you've suggested. I think you're right. It's going to be magnificent." She smiled warmly at Georgina and saw a little color return to the woman's face. Before any of them could respond, she continued, "I'll get started on the new designs right away."

Posie nodded goodbye at Georgina and R.C., then at Cleo, who was sitting so still and quiet Posie had almost forgotten she was there. Purposefully giving the elder Mr. Reynolds only a cursory look, she started the long walk across the ballroom to leave. She didn't know if it was possible for someone as rich, powerful, and mean spirited to feel snubbed by a lowly pastry chef, but she had tried her best.

Voices rose up again, but behind her this time. R.C. and his father in a near argument. The generational power struggle of a rich family playing out as she escaped the scene and made her way back to the kitchen. Posie shoved the ugly incident aside. She had her own mess to deal with now.

She needed to wrap her head around what to do to catch up with the new plan. Gingerbread city? Not her specialty. Her decorating tools would work on gingerbread just as well as they did on cake, but the cookie buildings were a whole other ball game.

Head down, wheels turning in her mind as she cooked up possible solutions to her dilemma, Posie wasn't watching where she was going. She stepped out of the ballroom, turned the corner into the hallway, and abruptly ran into someone.

"Oof!" All the wind left her lungs like she had been punched in the stomach.

She had run into a man. He grabbed hold of her arms to keep her from falling. "Posie!"

She looked up into his face, shocked. "Oliver?"

Oliver was still in his jeans and the heavy knit sweater he had worn to the stables with her, but he'd thrown a sport coat over the sweater. He still had on his glasses and he smelled like hay, fresh cold snow, and hot coffee.

Somehow, Oliver looked taller inside the mansion. More handsome, too. He also looked amused.

She blinked up into his face and watched as a smile spread across it, increasing his good looks tenfold. His eyes connected to hers, a sparkle lighting them up like he was pleased to see her, might laugh out loud, or perhaps even kiss her right there on the spot.

Posie's heart skipped a beat.

"Oliver!" A harsh voice from nearby broke their connection.

They both turned to see R.C.'s father, Oliver's grandfather, standing ominously in the entrance to the ballroom, glaring at them. He spoke in a slow, icy tone, enunciating carefully, "Unhand the help, Oliver. Immediately."

Anger flushed Oliver's cheeks, but he released his hold on Posie's arms without a word, dropping his gaze to the floor as he did.

Grandfather Reynolds observed his grandson with a cold eye then flicked a dismissive glance at Posie. He sniffed. "Now, come with me. We have a meeting at ten with Mr. Danbury." He gave Oliver's attire a scornful look. "Dressing to impress once again, I see."

Posie's own cheeks flared red on Oliver's behalf, but

Oliver kept his eyes averted to the floor, not daring to look at his grandfather or her. She bit her lip and kept her mouth shut. It wasn't her place to snap at her client's father-in-law, no matter how badly she wanted to.

Back in the kitchen Posie had to push all of her interactions with the Reynolds family, including the more pleasant interactions with Oliver, to the back of her mind. She had a lot to do. First was to inventory all of the equipment and tools she would need to make and decorate a ton of gingerbread over the next several days.

"We'll send someone to get more baking sheets and whatever else you need," Rafael told her over a quick lunch of turkey croissant sandwich in the kitchen conservatory. "Can you get me a list?"

"Yes, I'm working on one right now. I can have it ready in about an hour, if that works?" Posie answered.

"That'll be perfect." Rafael looked at the rest of the staff then gave Posie a supportive smile. "And Posie, we'll do everything we can to help. Don't be afraid to ask."

"As long as it doesn't interfere with your other duties," Margaret added. She had entered the kitchen while they were eating lunch and stopped at the head of the table to give them all a strict look.

Posie gave her a thin smile and basically lied. "Of course, I don't think I'll need much additional assistance." In truth she had no idea how much extra help she might need.

Posie didn't feel much better at the end of the day. With Rafael's help and Rafael Jr's afternoon run to get extra supplies, she believed she had what she needed to get the job done. But she still didn't have the designs.

She had tried to work on some sketches in the conservatory, but hadn't come up with anything amazing. All that kept running through her mind were images of regular old gingerbread houses and Posie knew Georgina wouldn't be impressed with anything run of the mill.

She excused herself early from dinner to go to her room and look up ideas on her cell phone. Maybe she just needed some inspiration to get her creative juices flowing. With a cup of clove tea from the kitchen, phone in hand, she relaxed into the armchair in the corner of her room, searching the internet.

She was so caught up with the task at hand, she didn't notice the new addition to her room until she went to bed.

Exhausted, her brain fried from trying to think too hard all day, bundled up in her snowman pajamas and ready to fall asleep, she reached out to turn off the lamp. Posie stopped suddenly, surprised at what she saw sitting on her nightstand.

A glass domed horse and sleigh clock shone merrily on her nightstand. The very same clock she had admired in Oliver's living room.

CHAPTER 7

"Paris!?"

Posie thought her brain might explode. Georgina's never-ending flow of ideas were driving her crazy. The last one, the final blow to Posie's barely manageable sanity, had been delivered via text message.

I know! Let's not just do any old city. Let's do Paris! It's perfect! Paris at Christmas time AND it's where R.C. and I spent the first few weeks of our honeymoon! That's what I want for the party. Christmas in Paris!

Posie felt all of the color leave her face. She stared at Cleo sitting next to her at the table in the conservatory. Piles of discarded gingerbread city plans were scattered across the surface of the table in front of them, all of which had become null and void with Georgina's final earth shattering text.

"Paris? How am I going to recreate Paris? I've never even been to Paris!" Posie lamented.

"I have!" Cleo offered eagerly.

Posie looked at her unassuming assistant. Maybe she would turn out to be useful after all.

Cleo's nose wrinkled. "It was kind of smelly."

"Perfect." Posie dropped her forehead onto the tabletop. She was beyond crying, having hit a new level of desperation even before Georgina's request for Paris.

Up before dawn, just like the day before, but this time spending every moment in the pre-light of morning hunting down the best gingerbread recipe she could find. It needed to have great flavor, but also the right consistency to build with, not too soft, not too heavy, and hard without being brittle.

By the time Posie made it down to the conservatory to meet Cleo and sketch out the plans, she was already drained. Armed only with some paper and pencils, an eraser, and the best gingerbread house recipe she could find on short notice, she had sat down with Cleo by her side to come up with the designs.

But building a gingerbread city required measurements and numbers, drawing to scale, and understanding how much weight any given gingerbread wall could sustain. She didn't have the proper drawing tools, let alone the know-how. Her specialty was large cakes. Three, four, sometimes as many as ten tiers high. Some of that knowledge could be transferred to a gingerbread city, but she wasn't confident it would be enough.

Posie kept her forehead on the table and groaned, "Now Paris. I'm going to have to make an Eiffel Tower."

Flanked by Junior and Althea, Rafael stood next to Posie and gave her a sympathetic smile. "Is there anything we can do to help?"

Posie lifted her head and managed a weak smile. "No, thank you. I appreciate your offer, but you have enough to do." This was more than true. Special guests of the Reynolds family had already started arriving to spend the holiday at Long Point. She only had one thing to figure out, Rafael and his staff had three meals a day to worry about. She mustered up a brighter smile for them. "I'll figure it out...somehow..."

She let her eyes drift across the discarded plans, holding back a sigh.

"Um, excuse me." A voice came from kitchen door. All eyes turned to see who it was.

"Mr. Oliver!" Rafael, all smiles, moved to greet Oliver as he entered. "What can I get for you this morning? Coffee? We have some lovely cinnamon crisp coffee cake."

"No, thank you, Rafael." Oliver returned the chef's greeting with his own warm smile. Then he glanced into the conservatory, finding Posie in her barely controlled state of dismay. "I was actually hoping to talk to Posie."

All eyes now turned to Posie and she felt her cheeks grow hot under the unexpected attention. Rafael ushered Oliver to come in and she stood up, knocking some of her drawings onto the floor.

She bent to pick them up, but they had scattered quite a ways, floating on the warm sweet air of the morning kitchen. Oliver grabbed the few that landed near the huge island and joined her at the table. Posie remained standing awkwardly, pleased to see him in another one of his appealing sweaters, this one was navy, but not sure why he had come.

"May I?" He put his hand on the back of one of the kitchen chairs.

"Please, of course, it's your house." Posie sat back down in her chair, flustered.

Oliver grinned. "Well, not technically."

She shook her head, trying to remain professionally polite under the gaze of the rest of the kitchen staff, plus Cleo. "Right, that's right, you don't live in this house." Posie glanced at the others. Was it wildly inappropriate for her to know where Oliver lived? She wondered what they would all think if they knew she'd already been inside of his house...in her pajamas, no less.

Oliver, for his part, seemed pretty calm. He watched her

evenly with an amused twinkle in his eyes, waiting for her to stop fidgeting and return his look.

"I wanted to check and see if your new alarm worked out?"

Posie's mind flew to the horse and sleigh clock sitting on her nightstand in her room, which she had figured out had an alarm that played Jingle Bells. She smiled bashfully, knowing that her cheeks were turning pink. "Yes, thank you. That was thoughtful. One horse open sleigh...clever."

"I didn't want you to be wandering around at all hours in search of a lost cell phone." He shuddered and made a fake face of horror at Cleo. Cleo looked back at him, utterly confused.

"It worked perfectly fine. Woke me right up. And it's so beautiful." Posie couldn't help but compliment his choice in clocks. He had certainly loaned her a gorgeous one.

"Yes, it is, isn't it?" He smiled, pleased and, apparently, feeling a little silly. "Hagrid helped pick it out. He thought you might like that one. It's one of his favorites."

She laughed, relaxing a bit as the kitchen staff returned to their duties and stopped watching her and Oliver out of the corners of their eyes. Posie leaned over to see as far to the front of the kitchen as she could. "And where is Hagrid?"

Oliver made a slight shake of his head and tut-tutted. "He's not allowed in the big house. Too many run-ins with the psycho patrol."

A real shudder moved across Posie's shoulders at the memory of the German Shepherds.

Cleo nodded grimly, finally catching on to that part of the conversation at least. "Thor and Diesel are the worst."

"Aren't they just?" Oliver responded.

They all sat in silence for a moment, pondering the viciousness of Oliver's grandfather's guard dogs. Only the clinking of silverware, running of water, and sounds of chopping drifted over to them from where Rafael and his team were making lunch.

Oliver was the one to break the silence, speaking low enough that his voice didn't travel past the table. "I saw you in the ballroom yesterday."

Posie looked up, not knowing how to respond. She knew he had seen her. They had run into each other at the entryway.

"That was brave…what you said to my grandfather."

"Your grandfather?" Posie's heart beat hard in her chest. Not only at the mention of the tense exchange in the ballroom, but at the intimate way Oliver was speaking to her in a near whisper. It was almost seductive. Definitely secretive.

"Yesterday. I saw everything from the hallway." He gave her a mischievous smile.

Posie looked nervously at Cleo, not exactly sure how loyal she was to the leader of the Reynolds family. She tried to be cool. "I didn't really say anything to him."

"I know!" Oliver tried to contain his delight while still whispering. He drummed the top of the table quietly with the palm of his hand. "That's what was so perfect. Nobody's ever brave enough to ignore him."

Cleo giggled then clamped her hand over her mouth. Posie relaxed and shrugged. It hadn't been that big of a deal, really, but she was glad Oliver and Cleo appreciated her standing up for Georgina, even in a very small way.

"What are you working on here?" Oliver had finally noticed what was on the papers scattered in front of them. He picked one up and inspected Posie's attempts at drawing a gingerbread building in the shape of a state capital.

"They're just some ideas for the big dessert."

His brow furrowed. "You're making a Whitehouse cake?"

She smiled, but it was a stressed out smile. "No, well, kind of. It's not a cake anymore for one thing."

"I see that. It looks more like a construction project." Oliver picked up several more of the sketches including ideas she'd had for a city zoo and an apartment building.

"It's a gingerbread city," Cleo told him.

"Ah, I see." Oliver continued poring over the drawings.

Posie reached out and pulled the rest of the drawings back in front of her so she could make a stack of them and throw them away. "They're all null and void now. We have new and, hopefully, final instructions on what we're supposed to make."

Oliver looked up. "Oh? What is the final assignment?"

She couldn't keep the bite out of her tone. "Paris. We're supposed to build the city of Paris...at Christmas...out of gingerbread."

Oliver raised his eyebrows and nodded slowly, looking cautiously between Posie and Cleo.

"By Saturday," Posie added.

"So, the Eiffel Tower, the Louvre, Notre Dame?" he asked.

"Oh, jeez! I forgot about Notre Dame!" Posie's shoulders slumped in defeat. She took a deep breath and blew it out through pursed lips. "It's okay. It's going to be okay. I just need to get the design right and we'll get started."

Oliver watched her, concern in his eyes. "Will you need them to be lit up from inside or anything like that?"

"I don't know yet. Although, that would probably be nice. It needs to be, you know, a stunning and magnificent creation. That's what Georgina expects." Posie stood to carry the stack of papers to the trash and start again. She caught sight of Margaret entering the kitchen as she did.

The housekeeper brought her normal cloud of doom with her as she swept past Rafael and his team toward the conservatory. "What's going on in here?"

Posie hesitated, glancing down at the messy papers in her

hands as well as the few escapees that remained on the floor at her feet. "Um...we're just–"

"Miss Miller, this kitchen facility is for cooking meals for the family and their guests. It's not someplace for you to spread out your...what is that in your hand?" Margaret was almost past the island. Oliver and Cleo had remained out of her view where they were seated at the table.

"Drawings. Plans for the gingerbread city."

"Well!" The word came out of Margaret's mouth as a cough. "We can't have this sort of mess in a well run household. This is a kitchen, not an architect's office. It's not suitable for you to be..." her words trailed off when Oliver stood up and turned to face her.

"It's not a problem, Margaret." He smiled politely, but with little warmth. "Posie will be using my drafting tables and whatever else she needs to complete the plans for Mrs. Reynolds. At the carriage house."

CHAPTER 8

"I will?" Posie was stunned at Oliver's announcement, but found both herself and an equally surprised Cleo being bustled out of the kitchen by Oliver none-theless. All while Margaret smiled stiffly after them.

As they proceeded into the main hall to leave, Oliver leaned in towards them. Speaking in a conspiratorial whisper, he said, "Margaret's always been on Team Grandfather. I think she may be secretly in love with him." Cleo giggled, which only encouraged him. He pointed at Cleo as proof positive. "See? She thinks so, too."

Posie didn't know about that theory, but she was glad to be out from under the housekeeper's eye. The woman was intense. "She knows how to suck the joy out of a room, doesn't she?"

Oliver let out a laugh, a sound which came as a surprise to Posie and, by the look on her face, Cleo as well.

His laugh also surprised Georgina, who happened to be descending the grand staircase with a few well groomed women friends and overheard his merriment.

"What's got you in such a good mood, Oliver?" Georgina

smiled widely, wanting to be in on the secret joke. She quickly took in Posie's presence next to him. Then her gaze landed on Cleo. She hurried down the rest of the stairs to intercept them before they got to the door. "I'm pleased to see my beautiful *single* niece and my handsome *single* nephew having such a good time together."

Cleo blushed red over what was a pretty obvious insinuation that she and Oliver should be a couple. Jealousy pinched Posie's heart, but she kept a polite smile on her face. Georgina slipped a curious look at her, probably wondering why she had been let out of the kitchen.

Oliver cleared his throat. "I've got a few things I wanted Posie to incorporate into your..." he eyed Georgina's friends, considering if she wanted him to spill the beans to them or not. Deciding not, he went on, "Your *Parisian surprise* for the party."

Georgina's eyes twinkled at the thought. "Oh? That sounds delightful."

"It will be, but we've got to get to my workshop so I can show her." He put one hand behind Posie and one behind Cleo and steered them past Georgina and out the door.

Bothered by Georgina's words, Posie remained fairly quiet on the short walk to the carriage house. They all did. It was too cold to talk anyway, better to keep their faces wrapped under wool scarves than try to make small talk and get frostbit noses.

She felt a little better when Hagrid greeted them at the door. The warmth and beauty of Oliver's home had a soothing effect, lifting some of the stress off of her shoulders.

"Let me put some coffee on and then I'll show you to the workshop." Oliver went to the kitchen, leaving Posie and Cleo waiting with Hagrid in the clock filled living room.

Even though she had only been there once before, Posie

felt oddly at home. She stood in front of the Christmas tree, whose lights had been on when they walked in.

"He's got so many now," Cleo said, peering at the bird cage clock.

"Clocks?"

Cleo nodded.

Posie was a little surprised. "You don't come over here very often?"

Cleo shook her head 'no'.

"I guess that makes sense. Georgina and R.C. have only been married a few years."

"That's true, but we've been friends of the family since I was a little girl. I've spent a lot of time at Long Point, but hardly any time inside Oliver's house."

Posie didn't have time to think much about that information, because Oliver returned from the kitchen.

"That'll be done soon. I can get you settled in the workshop."

Posie didn't know what she had been expecting, though in hindsight she realized a normal person may have thought of the drafting table in Oliver's living room as a work space. That was, it turned out, only a teaser of the workspace he actually had inside the carriage house.

Three flights of stairs up, at the top of the house was a large open attic room that had been converted into a workshop like none Posie had ever seen. Or even imagined.

Heavy beams scored the peaked ceiling. Wood plank floors were sanded and stained, which surprised Posie. She had assumed when they started up the third flight of narrow stairs that the highest floor in the carriage house would be more rustic.

Though it kept some of what must have been its original rough charm with the floors and ceiling, there was also a wood stove giving off plenty of heat and two wrought iron chandeliers gracing the ceiling, one on each side of the room. They looked as if someone, Oliver she guessed, had built them out of antique fixtures he had found in the carriage house.

Besides all of this there were two drafting tables, three long work tables full of books and clocks and parts and tools, and in the corner a massive desk complete with rolling leather office chair. But none of these things compared to the windows.

On both end walls huge circle shaped windows designed to look like clocks watched over Long Point. Wrought iron made up the numbers and hands of the clocks. They weren't meant to actually operate, but were fit into the window glass for decoration. Glass so thick the view of the outside was distorted.

The windows made it seem as if they were inside of a clock. Posie knew without asking that Oliver had made them himself. He had turned his workroom into something approaching the fantastical.

"Wow." Cleo wandered to the clock window that over-looked the section of the grounds that led to the stables. Posie could tell by her reaction that Cleo had never been inside Oliver's workshop. She wondered if anyone had.

For Oliver's part, he was hurrying from table to table trying to straighten up. An impossible task, but charming to witness.

"So, I was thinking you could use this drafting table." He carried an armload of blueprints, or something like, from the drafting table in question and dropped them onto the nearest work table. He looked at Posie expectantly. "Do you think that will work for you?"

Posie moved slowly to the drafting table and sat down on the tall stool behind it. Remembering he'd forgotten some-thing, Oliver lunged forward and clicked on a flexible light that was clipped onto the side of the table and could be moved around into whatever position Posie desired.

She smiled at him. "I think if I can't create something amazing here, then I can't create it anywhere."

With a pleased smile Oliver breathed a small sigh of relief. As if she could have been disappointed in this place. As if anyone wouldn't be dazzled by the wonder of it. Though she supposed him inviting her and Cleo into his workshop was a lot like inviting them into his mind, maybe even his soul. That would make anyone nervous.

"I'll just look up the landmarks in Paris and I can transfer the images onto paper and create a template to work from," she thought through the steps out loud.

"Or!" Oliver held up one finger. "I have this too!" He bounded to a set of book shelves behind the desk and ran his finger along the spines of the tallest books held on the bottom shelf. "Here it is," he declared, pulling out what looked like a textbook from a Harry Potter movie. He held the book open on one arm and flipped through it hurriedly as he returned to Posie, plopping the book down so she could see. It was open to a page with a detailed picture of Notre Dame. "For reference."

Posie peered at the picture. "That's great, thank you, but I can probably find whatever I need on this." She held up her cell phone.

Oliver looked disappointed and gave her lukewarm shrug. "That could work, I guess. But it's so small."

Posie looked at her cell phone screen. It was pretty small.

"If you insist on using the internet, you can use my computer."

Posie looked at him with surprise. "You own a computer?"

He scoffed and gestured toward his desk. Posie followed his direction. Sure enough, buried behind a stack of books and other knick-knacks including a vintage metal scale, she could see the corner of a computer monitor sticking out.

"Well, what do you know about that?" she laughed.

Oliver put his hand on his heart like she had wounded him deeply. "I'm not a Neanderthal, Posie."

"I'll look up whatever you want on the computer," Cleo volunteered, sitting down at the desk.

"And I'll bring you what you need." Oliver placed several large pieces of paper, two rulers, and freshly sharpened pencils in front of Posie. "Starting with coffee!" He turned to go back downstairs.

Posie watched him leaving as Cleo moved the books on his desk so she could get to the monitor. She dropped her gaze to the empty paper in front of her and sighed. "And I'll start drawing."

Several hours and a few pots of coffee later, she had her plans for a remarkable gingerbread Paris at Christmas.

She had chosen five landmarks to replicate: the Eiffel Tower, the Arc de Triomphe, Notre Dame, The Moulin Rouge, and the Pont Alexandre III bridge. Then she completed her city scape with a Christmas street market, which included a merry-go-round and row of apartments with luxurious balconies overlooking shops and cafes on the street below.

It wouldn't be an exact replica of the city by any means, but she thought it highlighted some of the city's beloved style while giving enough depth to make it interesting. The streets themselves would be lined with trees and ornate street lamps, both made from either chocolate or fondant, she wasn't sure yet. She had decided to build everything from smooth flat gingerbread then utilize her cake decorating skills to add all of the fine details with white frosting.

"Do you want lights? Or movement?" Oliver asked as he looked over her designs.

She had thought about adding movement to the Moulin Rouge and the merry-go-round, and perhaps lights glowing warm from inside sugar paned windows in all of the buildings, and even little white lights on the trees and decorating the outside of the shops to go along with the white light theme at Long Point, but she didn't think there was time.

Posie shook her head 'no'. "I don't see how I can get that much done. I'll have to utilize table lights to illuminate everything."

Slightly disappointed, but respecting her decision, Oliver put the designs carefully down and clapped her on the back. "Excellent work. This will be the best gingerbread Paris anyone has ever seen. Now, how about some lunch?"

Oliver was a pretty good cook. While she and Cleo had worked upstairs he had put together a delicious white bean soup. And as they sipped mugs of clove tea at the kitchen island, he whipped up grilled cheese sandwiches using fat slices of bread cut from what appeared to be a homemade loaf.

"Did you bake this?" Cleo, a little in awe of his skills in the kitchen, held up one half of her grilled cheese sandwich.

"I did." He glanced at Posie then back to Cleo. "I usually don't go to the big house much, so I learned to fend for myself."

Posie had already taken a bite of her grilled cheese. It was perfect. Crispy brown on the outside, creamy and hot on the inside. The homemade bread was mouth-watering. "This is delicious," she said, still chewing.

Oliver sipped his tea, his eyes smiling at her enthusiasm over the rim of his mug.

"Is it because of Margaret?" Cleo asked.

Oliver turned his attention to her. "Is what because of Margaret?"

"Why you don't go to the main...the big house." Cleo

waited a few beats for an answer, then had a sudden realization. "Or is it because of..." She glanced at Posie, wondering if she should ask the question, then decided to go ahead. "Your grandfather?"

Oliver's face hardened. He stared down into his clove tea and Cleo gave Posie a slightly panicked look. Posie swallowed her bite of grilled cheese, not sure what to say to ease the sudden tension.

"Not that you have to tell us," Cleo tried to backtrack.

Oliver squeezed his eyes shut and did a quick shake of his head, as if he was trying to get rid of a thought. Or several thoughts.

He looked up at both of them and forced a smile. Posie could see a lot of pain under that smile. Her heart went out to him over her bowl of white bean soup.

Cleo, deeply bothered at having brought it up, said, "I shouldn't have asked."

"No, no, no, it's fine." Oliver shook it off and offered them a brighter, more mischievous smile. "Of course anyone who knows Margaret would assume I would do everything in my power to avoid interacting with her." He shook his shoulders in a comical shudder, making Cleo giggle.

"Do you really think she's secretly in love with your grandfather?" Posie blurted out the question before thinking, surprising the others and herself. It was one thing for Cleo to ask intimate questions about their family, but she was an outsider. She had only known them both for a couple of days.

Oliver looked into her eyes for a long moment. One of his searching looks that made her feel like they had a mysterious secret in common.

Finally, he cocked his head, his expression softening. "Actually, I do think so. Margaret's been working here ever since I was a child and I think I've always known she had strong feelings for my grandfather. After my grandmother passed, Margaret barely left his side." Oliver pondered what he had just said, then added, "Come to think of it, he didn't seem to mind. And he's always received Margaret differently than anyone else. Even his family."

"Really?" Posie found that part of his recollection especially interesting. In her few interactions with Oliver's grandfather, he hadn't come across as someone who would receive anybody well.

Oliver nodded, still musing. "I wonder if he has the same feelings about Margaret as she does for him." Cleo's mouth dropped open, making Oliver laugh. "My thoughts exactly, Cleo."

"That would be totally shocking." Cleo laughed.

Oliver shook his head, harder this time, laughing off the possibility. "No, that would be impossible. He would never. He barely looks at the staff as human beings, he would never fall in love with one. Would never allow..." Oliver's words trailed off as he, apparently, remembered Posie was a member of the staff. He cleared his throat. "Well, a life of unrequited love does explain her attitude I suppose."

"She really is...kind of...like a..." Cleo searched for the right words.

"A psycho-patrol?" Posie suggested, the image of Margaret guarding the house and Oliver's grandfather like the German Shepherd's guarded the grounds popping into her head.

Oliver and Cleo both froze and looked at her then each other. Then they cracked up laughing.

Posie laughed, too, though less noisily. The way Oliver and Cleo fell into each other while laughing made her stomach churn. Feeling like a 'member of the staff' trying to act like a real person in front of her boss' kids made her a little sick to her stomach. Or maybe it was the white bean soup.

Still chuckling, Oliver said, "It's not exactly her fault,

really. Grandfather does that to people. He has a way of backing people into corners and turning them mean."

Posie eyed him. "Sounds kind of cruel."

Oliver shrugged. "It's a family trait, I suppose."

She knew he was joking around, but Posie still didn't like the way Oliver was talking about himself. "You don't seem to be a mean person. Maybe you're more like someone else in your family. Your uncle, R.C. seems pretty nice. Or maybe your father?"

Oliver's shoulders stiffened and once again he averted his eyes, staring at the clove tea in his mug. Cleo shifted uncomfortably in her chair, avoiding eye contact with both of them. Posie wondered what boundary she had overstepped this time.

Oliver cleared his throat and spoke while still looking into his tea. "I didn't know them. They died when I was three. Plane accident."

There it was.

Their connection.

Oliver had lost his parents just like she had. The flashes of sorrow she detected whenever he looked into her eyes was a reflection of the particular pain she also felt. The pain of being utterly abandoned as a child by the two people who matter most.

Posie's throat clenched. She swallowed tears that were threatening to show up and embarrass her further. "I'm sorry. I didn't know."

Oliver brushed her apology aside. "I don't remember them at all. I was so young."

As if not remembering them was a reason not to be sad. If anything, it made the whole situation more tragic. At least she had memories of her parents, precious few that they were.

Posie opened her mouth to tell him about her parents. To

let him know she understood and that he could admit his feelings with her, she wouldn't judge. But before she could say anything, Cleo slid her hand across the table and put it on top of Oliver's. His fingers took hold of her hand and he looked up at her with a warm, sad smile.

Posie's stomach churned again as she witnessed their sweet exchange. How stupid could she be? Of course Oliver and Cleo were a couple, or well on their way to becoming one. Georgina had all but said so. All Posie was there to do was bake the fancy dessert for their party. She had no business at this table or in this conversation.

It didn't matter to her what was or wasn't going on between the two cousins-by-marriage. If this was a love story, it wasn't her love story. This was a gig she needed to finish in order to get paid and fix her life.

The planning was done. Lunch needed to be over.

Coming back to reality, Posie stood up abruptly, picking up her empty plate and near empty bowl. She went to the sink to wash her dishes and spoke over her shoulder. "I'm sorry to cut lunch short and I appreciate you letting me use your home to create my designs, but I really need to head back to the kitchen. I've got gingerbread to bake!"

CHAPTER 9

Armed with her designs, her love of baking, and a renewed dedication to get the job done and over with, Posie returned to the kitchen – with Cleo close on her heels. Regretting her decision to allow Georgina's niece to be her assistant, Posie tried to make the best of the situation.

A difficult challenge, given that Cleo was somewhat of a klutz in the kitchen.

The plan was to cut out the templates, roll out the gingerbread, cut the forms out using the templates, chill the cut gingerbread and bake them in shifts. Those pieces, which would comprise the walls and roofs of the buildings, would have to be left overnight to cool and they could begin assembly in the morning. At that point they could bake some of the finer items, like the Moulin Rouge windmill, the carousel horses, and the dreaded Eiffel Tower. If all went well, Posie figured she would have plenty of time to decorate the finished buildings before the Christmas party.

If all went well.

First things first, Posie baked a small test batch of the

75

gingerbread recipe she had chosen to ensure the flavor and consistency were right. Satisfied, she set about mixing up the first big batch, enough to fill four large baking sheets with cutouts, which went straight into the fridge.

"I'll take these," Cleo offered, grabbing the first two chilled baking sheets when they were ready. Eager to help, she moved too quickly and, with a sudden yelp, was suddenly sitting on the kitchen floor, both baking sheets plopped upside down on either side of her.

"Are you all right?" Posie, hands covered with cookie dough, moved to help her up. She glanced around as she did, wondering how in the world the girl had tripped.

Cleo waved her away. "I'm fine, I don't know what happened." She stood up and looked glumly down at the ruined dough.

"That's okay. It happens to the best of us," Posie reassured her.

"I'll get this cleaned up right away," Cleo offered.

Posie tipped her head at the two remaining baking sheets ready to go in the oven. "Why don't you pop those in first? You can clean up while they're baking."

"Okay," Cleo did as she suggested, moving painfully slow and careful this time. The sheets made it safely into the oven. Two sheets baking, countless more to prepare.

Pretty soon Cleo had tidied up the mess and the delicious scent of baking gingerbread filled the air. They had four more sheets ready when the timer went off telling them the first two sheets were done.

"I'll get them!" Cleo said, hurrying to the oven before Posie noticed she didn't have on any oven mitts. Cleo opened the oven door, snatched the baking sheets out and promptly dropped them onto the floor. "Ouch!"

"Cleo!" Posie hurried to her side and led her to the nearest sink to run cold water over the burns. "You can't touch something that's been in the oven without protection on your hands."

Cleo winced in pain, crestfallen at her mistake. "I'm sorry. I'm so sorry." She stared at the crumbled mess of hot gingerbread on the floor and her eyes welled up with tears.

"Now, now, don't worry about that." Posie's heart went out to her. How someone her age who supposedly loved baking didn't know the basics of cooking was beyond her understanding. She could tell Cleo was considering giving up.

As much as she might be able to move faster and more efficiently without Cleo's assistance, Posie couldn't ignore the heartbreak in the girl's eyes. She wasn't about to Grinch out and ban her from the kitchen.

"I think, before we get everything cranking on this gingerbread stuff, we should have a little kitchen safety review. Baking 101, if you will." Posie smiled her encouragement as she patted Cleo's hands dry with a clean paper towel and inspected the burns. "Not too bad. I've had worse." She pushed her palms forward so Cleo could see all of her scars. "I've been burned, cut, grated, sliced, and fried over the years. It's part of the territory. We just need to be sure we do what we can to not get hurt whenever possible."

Cleo nodded, sniffling.

They cleaned up the latest mess of gingerbread off the floor then Posie, donning oven mitts to show Cleo the best example possible, put the next four prepared sheets in to bake. After that she walked Cleo through kitchen safety rules and assigned a pair of oven mitts for Cleo to keep with her at all times.

"One of the most important things to remember, besides protecting your skin from hot surfaces and keeping knife blades pointing down and away from you and everyone else, is to remain calm and move carefully and purposefully. No rushing whenever possible. When we hurry, we risk slipping, falling, breaking, and burning, right?" Posie finished her tutorial with an bright smile.

Cleo nodded, a cautious smile returning to her previously sullen face. "Right. Got it."

"How's everything going, ladies?" Rafael and his team had returned to the kitchen to prepare dinner after their mid-afternoon break. He had witnessed the first unfortunate dropping incident before they left. Posie was glad for Cleo that he hadn't seen the second one involving no oven mitts. He may have banned her from his kitchen for something like that. She'd known chefs to ban people from their kitchen for less.

"It's getting going. We're beginning our baking assembly line." On cue, the timer went off to take their first successful batch of gingerbread out of the oven.

Cleo, oven mitts firmly in place, took out two of the sheets while Posie got the other two. The excitement the girl had for the process was unmistakeable. Though it pained Posie to admit it, she could see why Oliver liked her. When she wasn't shrinking into the background, Cleo was quite pretty and sweet.

Ugh. What was she doing worrying about why Oliver did or didn't like Cleo? She had more important cookies to bake and cities to build.

It didn't take long for Cleo to get the hang of moving the cutout pieces of gingerbread onto the sheets, placing them in the refrigerator, setting the timer, then getting them baked. Posie was falling behind on mixing batches of dough, rolling out the dough, and cutting the templates out.

"How do you feel about making the dough?" Posie asked Cleo, fighting down a sense of dread as she did.

"Could I?" The girl's face was so full of joy, Posie felt like she had just announced Cleo would be getting a pony for Christmas.

"Of course you can, I'll walk you through the steps."

It wasn't a difficult recipe. Eggs, sugar, butter then the dry ingredients. Posie had written everything about the recipe out step-by-step on a piece of paper that was now propped up on a recipe book stand in front of them. There was nothing complicated about it at all.

Posie showed her how to operate the mixer, emphasizing the dangers of the deceivingly powerful machine and how Cleo should absolutely never, under any circumstances, stick her hand or finger anywhere near the spinning beater.

"And once you're done mixing, you unplug it. Every. Single. Time. Do you understand? You are not to have it plugged in when you're tilting it up or at any time you're not literally using the mixer to mix. Got it?"

"Okay, got it."

"I'm right here so you can ask me anything if you get confused." Posie was, indeed, right next to the mixing station they had set up. Sitting only three feet away at the same counter while she rolled out dough, placed templates on the surface, and carefully cut out the shapes. There was no way Cleo could do anything and Posie wouldn't see it.

Actually, there was one thing.

Several batches into Cleo's first foray into mixing cookie dough from scratch, Posie glanced up from where she was cutting one side of the Arc de Triomphe and saw Cleo dump a heaping tablespoon of black pepper into the dough.

"Whoa," Posie said, startled at what she had seen. "What are you doing?"

Cleo froze, her eyes widening. "Putting in the pepper?"

"Yes, but how much pepper?"

The recipe Posie had chosen did include a tiny amount of black pepper. It was kind of a secret ingredient that added a spicy punch to the gingerbread. But it was only a tiny amount. A tablespoon was not a tiny amount.

"Four tablespoons?" Cleo answered with a whimper.

Posie's mouth dropped open. "Tablespoons!?"

It wasn't the end of the world. It wasn't even the end of a productive day of baking. But it was frustrating enough to make Posie want to let out an exasperated growl, but she didn't want to send Cleo into a downward spiral. From her slumping shoulders and crumpled frown, it was obvious the girl was already beating herself up over the mistake.

One of their most precious resources was time. Unfortunately, any mistake, no matter how innocent, cost time. Posie pinched the bridge of her nose and squeezed her eyes shut.

"I'm sorry, Posie. I thought that's what the recipe said. I'm not very good at this, am I?" The tone in Cleo's voice snapped Posie out of her own misery.

Insecurity, not feeling good enough, being unworthy and forgettable, was what she heard in Cleo's voice. She refused to be party to putting that kind of negativity onto somebody else, no matter what they had done to her gingerbread recipe.

Posie pulled her hand down her face, wiping away her initial response. "No, it's not that you're not good at it. Anyone can make a mistake. We just need to figure out how far back the mistake went and fix it."

It went back three full batches. Over a dozen sheets full of gingerbread. It was going to be a long afternoon.

In Cleo's defense, Posie's scratchy handwriting could be confusing. And she hadn't really written the recipe out thinking that someone else would be reading it. Plus they had been doubling the recipe, and that could be confusing to a novice. The blame for the mistake could be spread between them and it was fixable.

"It's just going to take a little longer to finish," Posie explained as she dumped the peppery gingerbread into the fast filling trash can. At this point they had thrown away more gingerbread than they had finished.

Cleo stared dismally into the trash can. "Will we get it done?"

Posie coughed out a laugh and put her arm around Cleo's shoulders. "Will we get it done? Of course we'll get it done! We always get it done."

"That's the spirit," Rafael called out from the stove where he was adding fresh crushed garlic to some olive oil. He waved at Junior. "Make these ladies a nice espresso. They need a little pick me up!"

The strong drink did pick them up and they got into a groove, baking until nearly midnight with only a 30 minute break to eat the dinner that Rafael served the staff.

At the end of the long afternoon, and even longer evening, they had finished all of the gingerbread needed to create every building and the bridge for their version of gingerbread Paris, three times over. Posie knew they would need backups for any breakage during assembly. Plus she liked to keep a full set of backups on hand, just in case. They wouldn't be assembled or decorated, but they could be if an emergency arose.

By the time she retired to her room Posie was exhausted. After a quick shower she checked her phone and saw that Bella had called. She flopped onto the bed and called her back.

"How's our friend Georgina?" Bella asked.

"Georgina's fine, mostly because she hasn't been coming around. After she changed all of our original plans she kind of rode off into the sunset."

"What plans did she change?"

She proceeded to explain to Bella about the gingerbread city, how it had to be Paris, and how Georgina had assigned Cleo to help her, who had next to no experience baking or even being in a kitchen.

"Oh my," was all Bella said. She didn't need to say more. Posie knew she understood the challenge.

"Yeah, tell me about it." Posie stretched and rolled over onto her side to be more comfortable. "I'm exhausted."

"But you were able to make all your templates?" Bella tried to be positive.

"Yes, all except for the Eiffel Tower. I'm going to work on that tomorrow after we assemble all of the buildings." Her eyes rested on Oliver's clock ticking away the seconds until midnight.

"That should put you in pretty good shape to be ready for the party?"

Posie yawned. "Yes, I think so."

"So maybe you'll be able to do something festive up there instead of working yourself to the bone?"

Posie chuckled. Bella was one to talk. She had a habit of falling into crazy holiday work schedules. "You know how it is, Bella. Work first. Play later."

"I'm sure you'll get the work done. You're brilliant at what you do, you know. I'm more concerned that you have a little fun at Christmas."

Posie's eyes lingered on the horse in the clock, its shining legs clicking back and forth, and she wondered what Oliver was up to in his workshop. If she wasn't so tired she might have gotten up to look out of her window to see if she could see light spilling out of the third floor clock windows.

But she was tired. And she was pretty sure he and Cleo were an item, or soon to be item. The only thing Posie needed to do was get some sleep so she could wake up refreshed the next morning and be brilliant.

CHAPTER 10

The only thing more stressful than glueing the walls of a gingerbread Notre Dame together with frosting was glueing the walls of Notre Dame together with frosting under the scornful gaze of Margaret, or *Mrs. Scrooge* as Posie had taken to thinking of her.

"Is that edible?" Margaret watched as the frosting oozed out from between the joined walls and Posie wiped away the extra with a damp paper towel before it hardened.

"Yep, it's edible."

Margaret narrowed her eyes. She didn't believe her. Not that Posie cared if Mrs. Scrooge believed her or not. She did care that her presence was making Cleo nervous and, therefore, even more prone to accidents. She was having to keep one eye on the girl to make sure she wasn't touching anything vitally important while she assembled Notre Dame. Not an easy task on a normal day, let alone four days before what was referred to around the staff quarters as 'C-Day'.

Posie had climbed onto the heavy worktable to kneel next to her Notre Dame replica. This provided her with the best angle to complete the assembly without having to move the

gingerbread building any more than necessary. The less movement that happened before the frosting had time to set, the
better.

Margaret sniffed. "When will these larger items be taken
into the ballroom?"

Posie all but ignored the question until the last inch of
frosting was in place. Focusing on doing the job right was
how she was choosing to handle Margaret's negativity. A plan
that was only half working. Though her eyes were sharp and
her hands steady, Posie's stomach tensed up whenever the
woman came near.

She completed the last swipe of extra frosting from the
back left corner of Notre Dame and looked up at Margaret,
feigning cooperation.

"I don't think we'll be able to move anything until the
morning before." Posie smiled with cool politeness.

"Christmas Eve!?" Margaret put her hand on her sternum
and Posie wondered how bad she would actually feel if the
older woman had a heart attack. "You can't keep all of this
here for that long!" Margaret swept her arm through the air
encompassing all of the gingerbread in the vicinity. Which
was a lot of gingerbread.

Posie looked across the two work tables at the already
assembled Moulin Rouge, Arc de Triomphe, the bridge, the
Parisian apartment building and, now, Notre Dame. All of the
buildings were spread out far enough away from one another
that she could do most of the pipe decoration without
moving them, which was ideal. Piping could be messy and she
hadn't wanted to do anything except for the most delicate
work and final touch ups once the pieces were in place in the
ballroom.

"All of this," Posie enunciated each word for emphasis. "Is
exactly what Mrs. Reynolds has requested. We cannot hurry
the process without possibly damaging the buildings."

Margaret gave her a sharp Mrs. Scrooge glare, but kept her lips pressed together in silence.

"How's Paris coming along?" Oliver's voice interrupted their stand off.

If Posie thought her stomach had been tense with Margaret watching her every move, it was nothing compared to the way the whole middle of her body tightened at the sound of Oliver's voice.

"Isn't it impressive?" Cleo was seated at the kitchen island where Posie had tasked her with rolling modeling chocolate into the shapes of tapered candles, which would be crafted into lamp posts.

"I would say so," Oliver agreed, taking in the gingerbread buildings with genuine awe. He caught Posie's eye. She was still perched on top of the table next to Notre Dame. "This looks amazing even without any decorations."

Margaret scoffed as quietly as someone like her could scoff, then excused herself to some other part of the mansion that needed her attention.

"Do you want some?" Cleo offered Oliver one of the pieces of gingerbread left over from the few pieces that had broken along the way.

"Thank you." Oliver took it and bit off a piece. His eyebrows lifted in surprise as he chewed. "And it tastes delicious, too."

Posie couldn't help but be pleased at his reaction. "Help yourself to anything in that pile."

He picked up another hefty piece. "Why thank you, I don't mind if I do."

"Don't give any of that to Hagrid, though," Cleo warned him. "Posie says it's not good for dogs to eat."

"I think it's the nutmeg," Posie added.

Oliver swallowed his second big bite and shook his head 'no'. "Hagrid doesn't like gingerbread anyway."

Posie was surprised. "You've given it to him?"

Oliver smiled. "He got into some Christmas cookies once, but he voted no on the gingerbread."

"Smart dog." She stood up, ready to move carefully around Notre Dame and climb down onto the floor. Instantly, Oliver was at the table offering her his hand. Feeling slightly silly, but grateful, Posie took his hand and immediately wished she hadn't.

Oliver's hand was warm and strong. Gentle, but capable. His gallant gesture of helping her descend from the work table only made her attraction to him rise to the surface again.

When she reached the floor safely, she pulled her hand away and said as cool and polite as she could, "Thank you."

"You're welcome." Oliver bit off another piece of ginger-bread, his eyes twinkling.

"What are you doing over here?" Cleo asked from her seat at the modeling chocolate station.

Oliver mocked feeling hurt at her question. "You don't want to see me?"

Cleo giggled. "You know what I meant. You never leave the carriage house unless you have a reason."

Oliver dropped his eyes to the floor and shoved his hands in his pockets. When he did look up, he directed his look at Posie. "I wanted to know if you might have time to take a break this afternoon."

Posie hesitated, glancing at Cleo. What was he doing? "Um, I don't know." She looked around at the finished build-ings that needed to sit until at least the next morning before she could work on them. "I do need to bake the Eiffel Tower today."

Oliver nodded in understanding and looked between her and Cleo. "Well, and this is only if you can take a break in two or three hours, I was wondering if you might want to go riding with me. Both of you."

"Yes, that would be wonderful." Cleo's whole face brightened into a brilliant smile, then she looked around at all of the modeling chocolate and gingerbread buildings and her smile faded. "I don't know if we'll have time."

Posie's heart, which had at first jumped at Oliver's suggestion, softened completely at his and Cleo's steadfast expressions of support. It seemed they would bravely face whatever she determined to be the right course of action. Finish the baking and decorating or go for a ride on a beautiful horse through the winter landscape.

There was no reason for them to worry that she would ruin the fun, however, because for Posie it was a no brainer.

Both.

"I need to bake the pieces for the Eiffel Tower first..." she let her words trail off as if she had to think really hard about what to do, then she beamed at them. "But we can get that done in three hours easy. I would love to go for a ride."

THE BRIGHT WINTER sun barely warmed Posie's cheeks and nose enough for her to keep them uncovered. Her fingertips were cold inside of the leather riding gloves Cleo had loaned her and she had lost nearly all feeling in her toes, but she didn't mind one bit.

Sitting on top of Honeycomb, whose smooth muscled body moved gracefully beneath her, Posie was having the time of her life. Thrilled to be in a saddle again, riding a horse after so many years, all worries about gingerbread Paris and the money problems at her bakery disappeared. All Posie could think about was the gorgeous horse beneath her and the equally gorgeous winter landscape of the Long Point estate.

Well, if she was being honest, there was one other thing she couldn't stop thinking about.

Oliver rode next to her, sitting tall and strong on Neptune, an impressive pure black stallion. He had insisted on her taking Honeycomb out even though Posie knew he rode her regularly.

"I saw how you looked at Honeycomb the other day," Oliver told her with a smile when they reached the stables and Finn was gathering their horses for them. "I insist you ride her today. Besides, she's the most well mannered of the bunch, except for Candy over there."

Candy was a small, slender bay and Cleo's normal mount. Cleo was in an especially good mood when they arrived at the stables. Probably happy to be out of the kitchen for a while on such a beautiful winter's day.

Finn, Posie noticed, took special care in delivering Candy to Cleo. "Here you are, m'lady."

Cleo blushed under the flirtatious eyes of the handsome stable manager, and allowed him to give her a quick boost up into the saddle. Posie looked to Oliver for his reaction. Finn's interest in Cleo seemed especially personal and she wondered if it bothered Oliver, but Oliver wasn't paying any attention. He was running his hand down Neptune's front right foreleg.

"He's well enough to ride?" Oliver asked Finn.

Finn left Cleo on Candy and joined Oliver at Neptune's side. "He is, sturdy as ever he was. Cleared by the vet yesterday."

Oliver stood and patted the horse firmly on his ebony neck. "We'll take it easy today anyway."

"You're wise for that, Mr. Oliver. Better to go a little slow in the beginning." Finn agreed.

Not much more had to be done, just mounting their steeds and guiding them through the stable doors and down the lane leading out to the open areas of the estate. Posie marveled at what a simple act it was, riding a horse, yet there was so much involved in getting there. The land, the stables, the saddles and bridles, the feed, the veterinarian visits, not to mention the clothes needed to stay warm. No wonder this was a sport available mostly to the wealthy.

Nothing about the experience was lost on Posie. The sound of hooves crunching through the hard top layer of snow, the sunlight glittering like diamonds across the unspoiled snow surrounding them, the jingling of bridles, the gentle snorting breath pluming great clouds of steam in front of the horse's noses. Her own nose, close to freezing in the crisp cold air, breathed in all of the smells of the horses, the outdoors, her warm wool riding clothes, and the leather saddle underneath her.

"Let's go to the ridge," Cleo suggested, turning Candy up a small slope to their left. Second guessing herself, she looked over her shoulder at Oliver. "Can Neptune make it?"

In answer to her question, Neptune shook his head sending his shiny black mane flowing through the air. Oliver laughed. "I think he's insulted by the question. Of course he can make it."

Posie followed the other two up the slope, carefully guiding Honeycomb, who was channeling her own gentle assurance back to her through the reins. She could almost hear the horse saying, *It's all right. I'll keep you safe. Just hang on and trust me.*

She remembered that feeling. Knowing someone bigger and stronger was looking after you and would never let you fall.

As she and Honeycomb arrived at the top of the ridge and stopped next to Oliver and Cleo who were looking at the view, memories of her parents came to Posie's mind. Their smiling, proud faces watching her ride another buckskin horse in another life a long, long time ago. Always cheering her on from the sidelines. Strong. Steady. Forever.

Or so she had thought.

Before Posie could stop them, hot tears welled up in her eyes and rolled quietly down her cold cheeks, instantly making them colder. She tried to swallow any further tears and sniffled hard before her nose could start running. Crying wasn't the best move on a frosty afternoon ride in the country.

"Are you all right?" Oliver had shifted his attention from the view to Posie.

She sniffled again, cleared her throat, and tried to sound normal. "It's the cold. It's making my eyes tear up," she lied.

Oliver watched her for a long moment. Neptune shook his great head as if he didn't believe her story either. Oliver pulled a clean white handkerchief out of his breast pocket and handed it to her.

Again with the Jane Austen vibe. Posie almost refused, the hanky bit was ridiculously gallant and old fashioned. Then she realized she had nothing to wipe the wet tears off of her face. If she let them sit there, her cheeks would be chapped and burning bright red by the time they returned.

"Thanks," she said quietly, taking the handkerchief from his gloved hand.

"We'll turn back," Oliver announced. "The temperature's dropping and I think this is enough for Neptune today."

Finn met them at the stable doors. "How was your ride?"

"Good, really beautiful," Posie answered. Finn nodded his approval and moved in front of her to take hold of Honeycomb's reins.

Before he could do so, however, Oliver dismounted and pushed Neptune's reins into Finn's hands. "He'll need a good rub down I imagine. So his leg doesn't get sore."

"Yes, sir, I'll get right on that." Finn took Neptune and

walked him toward his stall, striking up a friendly chat with Cleo, who was already leading Candy to her stall.

"Allow me." Oliver moved to Honeycomb's side where Posie was about to dismount.

"I think I can do it by myself," Posie protested mildly.

He grinned up at her. "I'm sure you can do it by yourself, but please, allow me." He took hold of Honeycomb's reins with one hand and stood ready to assist Posie as she got off the horse.

His offer to help wasn't quite so silly when Posie moved to swing her leg back and over Honeycomb's rump and dismount. Her own rear end and inner thighs were stiff and suddenly not following direction. She grunted in pain.

"It's not unusual to get quite sore after riding for the first time in a long time." Oliver explained the reasoning behind his chivalry.

"Yes, I see that now." Posie grunted again as she forced her body to follow directions and got both of her legs into place so she could step to the ground, which seemed a lot farther away than when she had climbed into the saddle.

Sensing her instability, Oliver reached up with his free hand and grasped her elbow. "I've got you."

With Oliver's support, Posie managed to drop fairly gracefully to the ground and stand on her own two feet. She turned to face him and thank him for his help, but was unprepared for how close together they were standing.

Looking up into his eyes, those searching eyes, Posie's mouth went dry. A flutter moved through her chest. She tried to gather her thoughts enough to say something polite and thank him for taking her for a ride, but before she could do any of that Honeycomb shifted her bulking frame behind Posie, knocking her off balance and unceremoniously pushing her into Oliver's chest.

"Whoa," he said, letting go of Honeycomb's reins and grabbing for Posie's waist with both hands.

It was too late. Their bodies were pressed together. His hands were around her waist. His gaze held her frozen in place.

The flutter in Posie's chest moved through her whole body. She couldn't get past the feeling of his body next to hers. Strong. Steady.

Forever. The word echoed through her mind.

Neither of them moved. The heat from their touch was already warming Posie's frozen cheeks, fingers, and toes. She could feel her heart pounding in her chest. Or was that his?

Without moving away from her, his hands growing even more firm on her waist, he spoke, his voice low, "Are you all right?"

She nodded, but she knew it was a lie. Warm in his steady arms, her heart longing for him to never let her go, Posie Miller was, most definitely, *not* all right.

CHAPTER 11

Compared to the hustle and bustle of Long Point's kitchen, the empty ballroom felt especially quiet. Even distant muffled sounds of activity in the halls outside barely penetrated the blanket of silence that the opulent space rested on Posie, soft and heavy.

If she had remembered her cell phone she could have slipped her ear pods in and at least had music to accompany her work. But her cell was still in her room, left behind after a fitful night of sleep and the urge to get up early and start decorating as soon as possible.

When she got to the kitchen she had decided she didn't want to cope with Margaret's nagging about her gingerbread buildings taking up so much room. Luckily, Junior had been up early as well and helped her move the Arc de Triomphe and the Moulin Rouge into the ballroom. They would need more people to move Notre Dame and the other larger more awkward pieces, but Posie could start with the first two.

All she wanted to do was decorate and lose herself in the process. The concentration of piping the smallest details was almost hypnotic and allowed her to forgot everything else.

And on this morning, all Posie wanted to do was forget.

She had taken a shower after the ride the day before then joined the staff in the kitchen conservatory for dinner. After that, Posie had spent all night assembling the Eiffel Tower, planning out and practicing all of the different decorating designs she would use on each of the gingerbread buildings, and attempting to wipe thoughts of Oliver out of her mind.

The only time she had managed to forget what it was like when he held her against him in the stable, the way her heart and his had seemed to beat together, the feel of his hands on her waist, the tingling that moved through her whole body when she looked into his eyes, was when she concentrated on piping. She figured with all the decorating needed to complete gingerbread Paris she could completely wipe any memory that Oliver Reynolds existed from her mind by the end of the day.

Cleo came plodding across the ballroom floor, looking for instruction. "What can I do to help?"

Posie, already deep in the decorating zone, really didn't want Cleo hanging around in the ballroom with her if she could help it. "Um, well, let's see. I already mixed up frosting. Probably as much as I'll need for a while. How are the lamp posts coming along?"

"I've finished all of them. Well, as much as I can without you." Cleo smiled sheepishly.

Posie considered the possibilities. Modeling chocolate was a good choice because Cleo had already been working with the medium and it required her to remain in the kitchen. "What about the trees?"

"The trees?"

Posie nodded. "We'll need at least a dozen trees of around the same height, though they can be different because they're trees and wouldn't be completely uniform anyway."

Cleo's brow furrowed with worry. "How do I make a tree?"

"Remember that wire I showed you?"

Cleo nodded. "Yes."

"You bend that into the tree shape you desire, making sure it isn't too top heavy, then cover it with tinfoil and then mold the chocolate over that form. We don't need to worry about leaves because it's winter in our gingerbread city."

Cleo was still nodding, more slowly now because she was deep in thought.

Posie put her piping bag in its holder and stood up. "Come on, I'll show you."

"No, you stay here." Cleo said in a remarkably confident voice, for her. "I think I understand. I'd like to try to make one by myself."

"Oh, okay," Posie was surprised, and also a little relieved. "Are you sure?"

Cleo nodded, pleased with the idea. "I can bring the wire form in here for you to check, right?"

"Sure." Posie swept her eyes across all of the plain brown surfaces of the gingerbread buildings and chuckled. "I'll be here all week."

With Cleo busy and out of her hair, she turned back to her piping task with renewed energy. Even if Cleo's chocolate trees didn't turn out, Posie could remake them fairly quickly. They would be one of the last items placed into the city anyway. Plus with Cleo hands busy in the modeling chocolate she wouldn't be touching any of the gingerbread, which was more fragile and took a little longer to redo than a chocolate tree.

"See? It's all going to work out just fine," Posie said to herself as she picked up her piping bag and leaned in to the Arc de Triomphe to finish the first layer of minute roping border, which she would let dry before adding the next layer.

Footsteps sounded on the ballroom floor, but Posie was so enrapt with her task she barely noticed them. She didn't realize Margaret was standing behind her until her grim housekeeper voice barked out a question.

"Who authorized you to move into the ballroom?"

Posie jumped, barely pulling her piping bag away from the Arc de Triomphe in time to keep from ruining what she was working on.

She put one hand on her chest. "Margaret, you scared me to death."

Margaret scowled, not caring that Posie had almost squirted an ugly, unwanted blob of frosting onto the Arc. "Who authorized you to move into the ballroom?" She repeated.

For one instant, fear rose in Posie's belly. Had she overstepped the house rules and put herself in danger of getting sacked before getting paid?

Wait. No. She hadn't done anything wrong.

Posie furrowed her brow and gave her head a quick shake before answering, "You did. You wanted me to move out of the kitchen and stop taking up so much space." Posie looked around the massive, nearly empty, ballroom. "I'm not in the way here, am I?"

Margaret pinched her lips together and Posie couldn't help but feel a small sense of satisfaction at the red tint spreading across the older woman's cheeks. But before she could relish getting under Margaret's skin properly another more harsh and commanding voice came from the wide ballroom entryway.

"What is going on in here?" Grandfather Reynolds glared at them and Posie's stomach filled with fear once again.

Oliver's grandfather stormed across the shining marble floor, moving remarkably quickly and smoothly for a man his age. When he reached the banquet table, he stopped and took in the incomplete Arc de Triomphe and Moulin Rouge with disdain.

Posie cringed, wishing she had more of the piping done and that everything didn't look quite so plain and messy. She hadn't even attached the blades to the front of the Moulin Rouge yet.

"What is this mess?" Grandfather Reynolds directed his angry question at Margaret, completely ignoring the fact that Posie existed.

Margaret's face, which had been turning bright red, suddenly paled. She started to explain, "Sir, I–"

Grandfather Reynolds didn't wait for her explanation. "In less than a week we are having some of the most powerful and influential people in the world inside of this room, Margaret. We can't have this...this...*elementary school project* laying around. Do you understand?"

It was Posie's turn to turn red. Elementary school project? Seriously? Did the man have some kind of mental block about fine pastries and grand party desserts?

Hot anger poured into her veins, overcoming her fear of losing her job. She opened her mouth to defend her ginger-bread city, but didn't get a chance.

"Of course, sir, I understand." Margaret's demeanor had switched. No longer the austere housekeeper being dressed down by her employer, she seemed suddenly more gentle, more placating. "Everything will be taken care of."

Posie watched in confusion as a changed Margaret stepped toward Grandfather Reynolds and reached out, lightly touching his forearm. Her eyes shone and a shadow of what could only be described as a coy smile touched her lips.

As bizarre as the move was between an employer and employee, it seemed to work. The irate expression on the elder man's face softened and to Posie's surprise he did not brush Margaret's hand away from his arm.

Without looking directly into Margaret's eyes or at Posie, he grumbled, "Just see that it is."

Margaret nodded seriously and shot a meaningful look at Posie, which was lost on her. Posie had no idea what had just transpired between Margaret and Grandfather Reynolds, but they walked out of the ballroom together leaving her with a strange sensation that she had just witnessed a secret.

Posie shuddered, the whole scene had been off putting. Grandfather Reynolds' words still rang in her ears, *elementary school project*.

Posie grunted. "What a jerk." She picked up her piping bag to get back to work, but try as she might she couldn't shake the anger that his disdain had brought up. She plunked the piping bag back into its holder. "I mean, who does he think he is?"

She scanned the incomplete Arc de Triomphe and Moulin Rouge, wishing again that they had been put together enough to impress him. Imagining his reaction when he saw the final results at the Christmas party, Posie felt a twinge of insecurity.

Would he still think the whole project was ridiculous? Did it matter? As long as Georgina liked it, Posie would get paid.

She sighed, frustrated.

Getting paid was important, for sure, but she didn't like the idea of anyone not walking away from one of her desserts without being impressed.

She turned and stared at the entryway where Margaret and Oliver's grandfather had just disappeared and narrowed her eyes. Her jaw setting with determination, Posie spoke under her breath into the empty ballroom. "He won't know what to think when I'm done. This is going to be the best gingerbread Paris anyone has ever seen. Better than Paris itself."

She pushed away from the table and strode quickly across the floor.

Soon she was standing at the front door of the carriage

house. She reached up and rapped firmly on the door, still fuming about Grandfather Reynolds' insults.

Oliver opened the door, casually appealing in a pair of dark jeans and an untucked business shirt. His eyebrows raised in happy surprise at her presence. "Posie, to what do I owe the—"

"You were right," she interrupted, trying to ignore the way her heart twirled inside of her chest at the sight of him.

He pushed his glasses up his nose then tilted his head to one side, curious. "I was right?"

Posie nodded. "About adding lights to the gingerbread city. I want to add lights...and music and whatever else we can think of to make it amazing. Will you help me?"

CHAPTER 12

"Is this what you want?" Oliver switched on the string of mini lights he had painstakingly placed inside of the previously assembled gingerbread Eiffel Tower. The lights blinked happily, giving the whole structure surprising elegance since it was still plain brown gingerbread.

Posie looked up from where she was piping decorations on Notre Dame. "Oh, that's perfect!"

Oliver grinned. Pleased that she was pleased, he stepped back and looked at what they had already completed.

Posie had to suppress a giggle. He wore a magnifying eye piece that was attached to a wide piece of leather strapped around his head. Apparently it helped him see the tiny lights better. He had flipped the eyepiece up to talk to her, but was still putting out quite a young mad scientist vibe. She managed to keep her amusement under wraps, not wanting to offend him. He had offered his assistance to save the day, after all.

With his and Cleo's help, Posie had moved all of the larger gingerbread buildings to the banquet table in the ballroom. While she piped frosting, Oliver had worked on the lighting for gingerbread Paris.

They had decided to use a no-heat normal sized light inside Notre Dame, which, when switched on, would shine warmly through the windows. That way Posie could start decorating the large building while Oliver did more precise lighting on the other structures. He had started with the Eiffel Tower.

He crossed his arms over his chest and put one hand on his chin, contemplating what he had accomplished so far. "You sure you like it?"

"I love it!" Posie was certain the detailed lighting would take gingerbread Paris to a new level. That confidence and working alongside Oliver all morning had brightened her mood considerably.

Oliver smiled, which made his eyes twinkle. Posie had to turn her attention back to Notre Dame to settle the flutter in her heart. She found his presence both exhilarating and distracting, and this was no time to be distracted.

"I've been thinking." Oliver went to the section of the table where Moulin Rouge pieces were still spread out, waiting to be assembled. He carefully picked up the famous blades of its windmill. "I can make this turn. If you want."

Posie paused her decorating. "You can?"

Studying the windmill blades he nodded. "Absolutely. Don't you have a carousel, too? I could make that turn as well."

Posie suddenly felt light, almost buoyant. As if she could float right into the air. "That would be amazing."

Oliver looked at her, beaming, and her heart brightened. Gingerbread Paris was going to blow everyone away, she was sure of it.

"There you are!" Georgina's voice carried easily across the

ballroom, interrupting the moment they had been sharing. She hurried across the floor, followed by a sheepish Cleo carrying a chocolate tree. "Oliver! I didn't know you were in here, too." Georgina gave Oliver's bicep an affectionate squeeze before artfully stepping aside so Cleo ended up standing next to him.

"Yes, I'm adding some extra light and mechanics," Oliver explained.

Georgina's gaze bounced off of his strange head gear and went right over his shoulder where it landed on the lit Eiffel Tower. She let out a loud gasp, putting her hand on her chest. "Oh my goodness! Posie, this looks gorgeous!"

"Thank you, it's not done...obviously."

"No, of course not, but I can see what you're doing here." Georgina scanned the table, lingering on the finished Arc de Triomphe. Then she covered her eyes with both hands and turned away. "No, no, no! I'm not going to look at it until it's done! I want to be surprised!" She reached out blindly toward Cleo and, finding the girl's shoulder, pushed her forward. "Show her what you made, Cleo."

Cleo held up a small, chocolate tree with bare branches. Her first. "I made a tree,"she said meekly.

Posie gave her a warm smile. "That looks great, Cleo. That's exactly the right size."

Still facing away from them and the banquet table, Georgina spoke into the empty ballroom. "I found Cleo working all by her lonesome in the kitchen and I thought certainly she could move out here and work with you."

A tiny stab of guilt made Posie wince. Not only had she enjoyed Cleo remaining in the kitchen because she couldn't do any damage to the gingerbread buildings from there, but her absence left Posie alone with Oliver, which she had been enjoying very much.

She cleared her throat. "Of course she can work next to

us. We'll have to move the supplies in here, but we have the room."

"Wonderful, let's do that right away." Georgina glanced sideways at Oliver. "It will give *everyone* a nice chance to spend time together."

Pushed by Georgina's heavy handed matchmaking, Posie, Oliver, and Cleo made their way through Long Point's long halls to the kitchen in silence. Posie wasn't sure why the other two weren't talking, but her own mood had nearly completely deflated since Georgina's interruption. She didn't feel much like talking as she thought about Oliver and Cleo's romantic relationship.

"I can't believe you're here in the big house with us so much over the holiday, Oliver," Cleo mused, gingerly balancing her chocolate tree in one hand while holding it at the tip with the other.

Oliver looked up and down the empty hall, pretending there was danger nearby. "To be honest, I'm supposed to be in a meeting with my grandfather and uncle. But I hate those meetings. And there is gingerbread to light up, which is a much more pleasant way to spend the day."

Cleo giggled, smiling up at him with admiration. Posie felt a little sick. She probably should have gone to the kitchen by herself to get the chocolate tree supplies instead of having to watch the kissing cousins moon over one another.

Male voices drifted down the hall. Irritated male voices.

They all paused.

"That will be them, probably looking for me," Oliver said miserably.

Cleo looked between him and Posie, alarmed. "If they make Oliver go with them he can't help finish Paris."

Posie also felt a growing sense of panic over the loss of his mechanical expertise. She'd had big plans to light up the little shops, the carousel, and the street lamps using Oliver's tools and knowledge. Without him the whole city was going to feel lifeless.

Oliver kept his eyes trained on the end of the hall where the men's voices were growing louder.

"Hide," Cleo said.

"Hide?" Posie asked. Not the most professional response.

Cleo motioned with the chocolate tree toward a long mirror hanging on the wall of the hallway. She widened her eyes at Oliver and whispered urgently, "Hide! I'll go get the supplies. We can meet back in the banquet room."

Understanding registered on Oliver's face and he stepped in front of the mirror, running his hand along the top right hand corner, feeling for something. Finding what he was looking for, his hand stopped.

There was a soft click then Oliver moved back and pulled open the mirror like it was a door, revealing the dim servant's hall behind the wall. He turned to them, gave them a gallant bow and looked up, his eyes dancing.

Cleo giggled again, but her merriment was short lived as the approaching voices grew louder. They were right around the corner and when they turned down the hallway they couldn't help but see them standing there with the mirror door wide open.

"Hurry!" Cleo whisper shouted.

To Posie's surprise, Oliver grabbed her by the hand and pulled her into the servant's hallway, leaving Cleo alone with her chocolate tree. He shut the mirrored door swiftly and they were alone in the dark. Well, not completely in the dark, there were the wall sconces, but compared to the brightly lit hallway, the sconces put off very little light.

"Why am I hiding? They're not looking for me," Posie asked, her dislike of the dark, narrow passageway taking over.

There was a long pause, then Oliver's deep chuckle. "I

don't know. I guess I panicked and yanked you in here with me."

"Terrific."

"Shhh..." Oliver moved closer. She could barely see him raise his finger to his lips. He whispered, "They'll hear you."

Sure enough, in the following silence Posie could hear the two men talking as they moved down the hallway. She could even hear the muted greeting of Cleo as she walked away and they passed her in their pursuit of Oliver.

"This is creepy," Posie whispered.

Oliver glanced around, nodding his agreement. Her eyes were adjusting so she could see him much better, though they were still very much in dim light. He looked back at her. Their eyes locked.

Posie stilled.

Dark silence surrounded the pool of soft light emanating from the wall sconce where they stood. Nobody could see them. Nobody could accidentally walk in on them. They were utterly alone.

All thoughts of gingerbread Paris and Grandfather Reynolds fell away.

Oliver's eyes searched hers, captivating her, making it impossible for her to move. Her heartbeat quickened. She held her breath. A hushed longing rose inside of her and, if she didn't know better, she swore it was mirrored in Oliver's gaze.

After a long...*long*...moment, something deep in his eyes shifted and he returned to their predicament.

He cleared his throat. "I guess we should try to find the ballroom."

Posie's eyes grew wide, a quiver of dread moving down her spine. "Try? You don't know how to get there?"

Amused, but calm, he reassured her. "I remember, it's just

been a while." He watched her reaction, which was less than calm. "There are lights the whole way. I promise."

Posie swallowed hard and made like she was braver than she felt.

"Here, so we stay close." Oliver reached out his hand.

She only hesitated for an instant, unsure if holding hands was a great idea or if it would only deepen her already thoroughly unprofessional attraction to him. But lurking around in the secret hallways of Long Point wasn't exactly professional either, so what did it really matter?

When she slipped her hand into his, Oliver smiled. A soft smile that barely touched his mouth, but shone in his eyes.

"Ready?" he asked, still whispering.

Another quiver moved down her spine, but it wasn't one of dread. She nodded. "Ready."

As he led her down the servant's hall, Oliver kept up a basically one sided conversation. She didn't know if it was for her benefit, to keep her from being afraid, or if he was settling his own nerves. Either way, it was the most she had ever heard him speak and she appreciated the effort.

"One of the young maids showed me these hallways when I was about seven. I had a terrible tutor that year, mean and unpleasant man. My grandfather hired him, if you can imagine. Anyway, one day when he was giving me a particularly harsh lecture she took pity on me and showed me how to duck into the servant's hall from the upstairs reading room next to my bedroom. She could see that I needed to get away from him...and others."

Posie imagined a seven-year old Oliver, orphaned and under the thumb of his grandfather, all alone in the vast mansion without a friend in the world except for a kind servant girl. The version of young Oliver in her mind wore big, awkward glasses. Very much the makings of a Dickens tale when she thought about it.

"What about Cleo? Did she spend a lot of time behind the walls?" For some reason Posie could imagine Cleo suffering under similar circumstances, being shy and awkward in a world full of Georgina's.

He nodded. "Yes, when she was here. Her family spent a lot of time at Long Point. They were old family business associates, you know what that's like." Posie did not know what that was like, but she kept quiet and listened as Oliver continued to reminisce. "Cleo hid from her mother and her aunt a lot. I hid from my grandfather. She was younger than me, but we used to sit on the floor with flashlights and play cards." He looked up at one of the wall sconces as they passed. "That's why I put these in, when I was old enough to do that kind of thing. I knew that Cleo, and I, and the servants used these passageways fairly often. I thought it would be less gloomy if there was some light."

"And how old was that? When you were old enough?"

Oliver's brow puckered as he thought back. "I think I was fourteen."

"Really? Wow."

He shrugged. "I've always had a knack for electronics and wiring. Fixing things. It's been a hobby of mine." He looked at her sheepishly. "As you could probably tell."

She laughed a little. "Yes, I've noticed."

They walked in silence for a few minutes. Posie lost in her thoughts about Oliver's childhood as he led her around several corners into a particularly narrow passage. He began counting wall sconces under his breath, stopping at number eight. He stopped so abruptly that Posie nearly ran into his back.

Oliver turned. He hadn't let go of her hand and their bodies were dangerously close.

"I think this is it." His voice was no longer a whisper, but still low and gravelly.

Posie gazed up into his eyes, unable to step back and give him space. She didn't want to give him any space. She wanted, in fact, to stay close to him. Get even closer. Wondered what it would be like if he tipped his head down and kissed her in this dark, quiet, secret place.

One corner of Oliver's mouth tugged up into a smile and his eyes twinkled mischievously. Maybe he was thinking the same thing.

Panic seized her and she pulled her hand out of his, blurting out the first thing that came to her mind. "Are you and Cleo...?" She paused, uncertain she should ask the question, but dying to know.

"Are me and Cleo what?"

"An item. A couple. In love since you were children. That kind of thing?"

"What?" Oliver coughed out a laugh and shook his head. "No! Not at all." He looked at her in disbelief that she would suggest such an extraordinary thing. Then a new look came across his face. Difficult to see in the dim light, but definitely there. An inquisitive look. As if he was fascinated that she had asked. He looked at her closely, his hand moving carefully up, like he was going to touch her cheek. He opened his mouth to say something.

A loud knock on the wall startled them both. Posie jumped and let out a squeal.

"Are you guys in there?" Though the voice was muffled, it was clearly Cleo calling to them. Who else knew they were inside the wall?

Oliver slowly tore his eyes away from Posie and directed his answer towards the wall. "Yes, we're here."

Posie took a few deep breaths.

Cleo had found them and interrupted the moment, but she wasn't Oliver's girlfriend.

And that changed everything.

CHAPTER 13

Posie returned to decorating Notre Dame with a light heart. Cleo set up her chocolate tree making on the far end of the banquet table. And, most exhilarating of all, Oliver stayed by Posie's side as he added beautiful lighting to her vision of gingerbread Paris.

"I didn't know you could do that with frosting." He was standing right behind Posie. The front of his shirt brushed against the back of her sleeve as he peered at the delicate piping work she was applying to the top of Notre Dome, a double rope pattern that literally hung free in the air like real rope.

The sensation of him so close didn't distract her, surprisingly. Instead it gave her a kind of super powered focus that made every flick of her wrist create the perfect frosting rope.

"It's all in the frosting," she said.

He grunted. "I'm pretty sure it's not just the frosting. You're very talented."

Pleased, Posie smiled, never taking her eyes off of the end of her piping bag, but remaining fully aware of Oliver's body behind hers. He literally emanated warmth. And he smelled good, too. She wondered what it would feel like if he were to wrap his arms around her from behind. A sudden rush of warmth rushed through her body and she had to pause for a microsecond before continuing.

Oliver leaned down even further, getting a better view of what she was doing. His breath tickled the back of her ear.

"Beautiful," he spoke so low he could only mean for her to hear.

Shivers rippled down her neck and across her shoulders.

Okay, now she was distracted.

"I think I'm done," Cleo announced.

She had completed two dozen chocolate trees, all approximately the same size and with just enough difference between them to look real.

"Very nice, Cleo," Posie was truly pleased as she looked them over. She wouldn't have to redo any of Cleo's work, which was a relief.

"Do you really think so?"

"Yes, you did a great job. I appreciate your help." Posie wasn't just trying to make her client's niece feel good, she knew that anything she didn't have to do, no matter how small, allowed her the time to make a truly amazing gingerbread Paris.

Oliver leaned down and inspected the row of chocolate trees. "I'm not the expert here, but I think they look fantastic."

Cleo brightened under their praise, then her face fell.

"What's the matter?" Posie asked.

Cleo's big eyes roamed over the gingerbread buildings, then back to her chocolate trees. "I guess I'm out of things to do now."

Posie laughed and placed her hand on Cleo's shoulder. "Oh, no, my friend. There is still plenty to do, let me assure you."

Oliver laughed too. A deep warm laugh. Once again he had positioned himself directly next to her and she couldn't bring herself to move away from him, even when their shoulders and arms touched. It was as if there was an invisible magnet pulling them together so every time they moved, they touched. Posie didn't know how to stop it, and didn't mind at all, so she didn't try.

She brought her attention back to the tasks at hand. "We do need to string the lights on the trees."

"I've got them!" Oliver left her side and went to the leather bag he had brought over from the carriage house. He rummaged through it and held up a handful of ultra mini light that were so small they merely looked like thin wire.

Posie shook her head. "I still can't believe you happened to have those in your house."

"You have no idea everything I've got jammed into my house. All of my years of hoarding the tiniest bits and pieces of metal and wire is finally paying off!" He placed the handful of micro lights next to the chocolate trees then dug out another handful of small white balls and put them on the table.

Posie picked up one of the balls, it was the size of a large marble, but was made of hollow plastic. "What are these for?"

Oliver ran his hand over hers to take the ball she was holding. He clicked something an unseen button one side of the ball, and it lit up. Returning it to her hand with a smile, he said, "I think these will work for the lamp posts."

"Those will be great!" Posie was delighted. "Do they run on batteries? How long will they last?"

"They'll run continuously for two weeks. Then they die, unfortunately. Which is why I never use them, but I think they might be perfect for this project."

"Agreed!" Posie was relieved she didn't have to figure out the lamps for the lamp posts, that was something she had put off hoping to come up with a brilliant solution. Lucky for her, Oliver had come up with one. "I guess we just need to figure out how to attach them to the top of our chocolate lamp posts."

"I'm on it! I'll go get the lamp posts from the kitchen." Cleo offered, so happy she had another important job to do that she practically bounced out of the room.

Posie watched her leave then glanced at Oliver before looking away quickly. A sudden timidness took over. She thought if she looked directly at him she might become so enrapt she wouldn't be able to look away. Ever. And that would not only be a little odd for the circumstances, but also unproductive.

Instead she chose to admire the gigantic Christmas tree in the center of the ballroom, staring at it as if it was the only thing grounding her in reality. Which, she supposed, it was.

Oliver cleared his throat. "Well, I think this is really shaping up. It's going to be a showstopper, that's for sure."

She felt rather than saw him step away from her and turn back toward the banquet table. She couldn't exactly remain staring in the opposite direction at the Christmas tree, besides she had work to do. Posie took a deep breath and turned to face gingerbread Paris with Oliver next to her.

She had to admit it was pretty impressive. Notre Dame had really come to life with the white decorations she was almost finished applying. The Arc de Triomphe was done, also with elegant white frosting. The fine decorative details in white against the gingerbread looked great and would be truly magical when she was finished. Even the undecorated Eiffel Tower looked impressive with Oliver's blinking lights.

The project wasn't done, by any means, but it was about halfway done and that was huge. She could finish the Eiffel Tower and the apartments and shops before the end of the day. That would put her in great shape to decorate the Moulin Rouge and the Carousel after Oliver completed his plans to add motion. That would leave her a full three days to add all of the little details and make sure gingerbread Paris was perfect.

Excited by that prospect and trying hard to keep everything professional even though she and Oliver were alone, she asked, "Do you think you could have the Moulin Rouge windmill and the carousel working by tomorrow morning?"

Oliver mirrored her seriousness by crossing his arms and giving her question a good think before answering, "Yes, I should be able to do that." He dropped his hands and picked up his leather bag, excited to show her something. "And I think you'll like this, too." He pulled out a small intricate device.

"What's that?"

"It's for a music box." He waited for her to respond. When she didn't, he continued while holding the gold music box player up closer for her to see. "I can add this to the turning device under the carousel...if you want."

"You can? What's the song?"

Oliver put his leather bag down and wound up the player, putting it carefully on the table when he was done. The cylinder turned and plinked out a light, thin tune. He grinned. "Dance of the Sugar Plum Fairies."

"Tchaikovsky! Oliver, that's perfect!"

Distracted by the sound of his name on her lips, he stopped and stared at her for a moment. Zeroing in on her. Sheer joy from making her happy shone in his eyes. Posie found she could not quite take in a breath under his gaze.

After a long moment he looked at the floor and cleared his throat. Without another word about gingerbread Paris, Oliver suddenly stepped away from the banquet table and faced her, standing at his fullest height before giving her a formal bow and holding out his hand. "May I have this dance?"

Posie's cheeks warmed, but she couldn't think of a reason to refuse. Especially with the way his eyes twinkled as he waited for her to respond.

She laughed then did her own mock stance of a regal lady ready to dance at a ball. Oliver's eyes lit up as she gave him her hand. He pulled her to him and out onto the dance floor, twirling her once for good measure.

She could not contain her smile and knew she was beaming up at Oliver as he swept her across the floor, humming along with Tchaikovsky tinkling from the table.

He was quite a good dancer. Better than her certainly. But Posie had learned to dance with her father when she was a little girl and he had always told her that she would be fine as long as she let the man lead.

Oliver was a good lead. The confidence with which he held her in his arms and moved her gracefully around the ball-room made it easier to follow him. Posie didn't mind not having to think about the dancing, she was too wrapped up in being so close to him and the sensation of his hands holding her.

Too soon the sound of the Dance of the Sugar Plum Fairies stopped. It took a few moments for both of them to realize it, but when they did they ended their dance. The silence left them standing somewhat awkwardly with each other, avoiding eye contact. Posie was surprisingly out of breath.

"I can fix that." Oliver tilted his head toward the silent music player. "Make it so it keeps playing."

"Good, good, that would be good." Posie couldn't think of one other thing to say. Cleo would be back any moment. She had to get back to work. She looked at Oliver and noticed his eyes were lifted up and he was looking at something over their heads. She followed his gaze.

Mistletoe.

Hanging from the chandelier above them was a bundle of mistletoe wrapped in a red ribbon. She sucked in her breath and dropped her eyes back to Oliver, who was now looking at her intently.

A thrilling tingle raced across Posie's skin. Every inch of her was wrapped in the excitement of what might come next. She blinked up at him, waiting.

"I think I got everything," Cleo said as she entered the room carrying a large shallow box.

Posie and Oliver startled and stepped away from each other. Posie put her hand on her chest, surprised at how her heart had jumped at Cleo's voice. Oliver ran his hand through his hair, leaving it messy and on end.

"Okay, well, we'll all get back to work then," Posie announced clumsily. She turned to go back to the banquet table, but Oliver touched her elbow halting her in her tracks.

Leaning down and speaking low so Cleo couldn't hear him from where she was depositing her box onto the table, he asked, "Would you like to go riding with me again tomorrow?" He glanced at Cleo and lowered his voice even more. "Just us?"

That night Posie was sticky from working with sugar all day and happy to take a shower. She was worn out, having gotten nearly the entire city of gingerbread Paris put together. But she was also pleased with their progress and was full of a solid sense of accomplishment as she got ready for bed.

She was also full of another kind of warm fuzzy feeling. As she snuggled into her bed and turned on her side so she could look at Oliver's horse and sleigh clock, she smiled.

The whole day had been a success, plus they hadn't had to

deal with Margaret at all, or Georgina, or Oliver's grandfather either, after they escaped into the servant's hall to avoid him.

Posie's heart fluttered in her chest at the memory of Oliver in the dark hall, Oliver on the dance floor, Oliver laughing and helping build gingerbread Paris. They had what amounted to a date to go horseback riding the next morning and she couldn't be more thrilled.

She drifted off to sleep with sugar plum fairies literally dancing in her head.

CHAPTER 14

The cold winter day was not short of sunshine. The bright sun took the bite out of the air and made for perfect riding weather. Posie sat astride Honeycomb, her body moving in sync with the horse's gentle stride. Oliver rode along next to them on Neptune. Both horses took their riders on an easy stroll along a dirt road. Hagrid was their joyful, if often elusive, companion. Jogging along beside them for a while then heading far away to run and bark playfully in the snow on his own.

Posie was glad she had taken the early morning off to go for a ride. Gingerbread Paris was almost complete and clearing her head in the fresh air was a good way to relax before she went in to make the final touches in the afternoon.

The two riders had enjoyed lively conversation on their morning outing. Covering topics such as their favorite movies, food, subjects in school and times of the year. They both agreed on action-adventure movies including fantasy and sci-fi. Italian food came in number one for both of them as well. They differed slightly on school subjects, Posie claiming history and English Lit as hers. Oliver agreeing, but adding in math and science as well.

"So...*every* subject was your favorite?" Posie teased.

Oliver chuckled. "I suppose, though I didn't like German very much. It made my throat feel funny."

Posie laughed. "I never took German. A little French, but not enough to get by in a conversation. Enough to pronounce food properly, though."

"Ah, that's mostly what you want to know when you're in France anyway."

"Have you spent much time in France? Paris, specifically?"

Oliver shifted in his saddle and turned his eyes toward the upcoming fork in the road. "Not too much."

Posie grinned. "Are you saying you aren't the best judge on whether or not my gingerbread Paris holds up to the real thing?"

He smiled and tipped his wool cap at her. "I can say that I've never seen a more beautiful cookie city than your gingerbread Paris at Christmas-time."

She laughed again. "And how many cookie cities have you seen, exactly?"

Oliver screwed his face up in mock concentration, pretending to count in his head before giving up and declaring, "So many, really. It's difficult to remember them all."

Posie didn't believe him and knew he didn't expect her to. "And do you like Christmas in general?"

He grew quiet and turned his attention again to the fork in the road, though he didn't seem to be seeing it. There was a far off look in his eyes as he answered, "Yes, I do."

Posie turned Honeycomb to go along with Oliver as he steered Neptune to the left at the fork. Their new path was just wide enough for two horses. Riding closer together gave her a good view of Oliver. She couldn't tell what he was thinking, whether it was good or bad or in between. But she sensed he was keeping something important under the surface and had to fight the urge to reach out and touch his arm in comfort.

Suddenly, he came back to the present, remembering she was right there next to him. He looked at her with a gleam in his eyes of someone intent on forgetting.

"What about you, Miss Posie? What's your favorite time of the year?"

Posie hesitated, wishing she was comfortable enough with him to ask if he was all right. But she wasn't. And she didn't. So she went along with his decision to continue their playful discussion.

"I've always been partial to fall, actually," she admitted, memories of past winters in tiny cold apartments in the city and wading through snow and icy slush to get to the subway for work flitting through her mind.

Oliver reined in Neptune, stopping his forward motion but not stopping the grand creature's hooves, which continued to step up and down on the frozen path in anticipation of moving forward. Honeycomb followed Neptune's lead, stopping without Posie guiding her.

Oliver's gave her a mischievous smile. "Well, then, I have a feeling we're about to change that." He swept his arm up and out, entreating her to look at the thick trees ahead that they were about to enter. "If you can go through the enchanted forest of Long Point without falling in love with winter, you are a stronger person than I."

Posie had been so distracted by their conversation, wondering what was going on in Oliver's mind, that she hadn't fully taken in the snow covered trees ahead of them. After Oliver called her attention to it, she couldn't pull her eyes away.

She would have thought a forest at winter might be a

gloomy place, dark and cold, somewhere to avoid until a warmer day. Long Point's forest was anything but that.

Trees reached high into the sky, some bare of leaves, some evergreen, all covered in snow. Bright blue sky showed above the quiet and undisturbed path they would follow. There was enough space between trees to allow sunlight to filter down to the snow covered ground.

The shadows weren't grey and gloomy as Posie expected, but a deeper shade of blue, beckoning them to venture further into the woods and look for deer or, perhaps something more mystical, like a winter gnome or Jack Frost himself.

A bright winter's day in blue and white splendor surrounded them as their horses stepped silently through fresh snow. Their rhythmic breathing created plumes of frosty air, the soft jingling of their reins muted by the peaceful majesty around them.

Enchanting. That's how Posie would describe the scene, but she didn't say what she was thinking. Speaking out loud in this beautiful place might break its spell. Besides, words would only fall short.

Oliver caught her eye. His black wool cap and jacket contrasted against the white and blue. Neptune's ebony coat shone underneath him. The ethereal light of the snow covered woods brought out every detail of them, horse and rider. Neptune's muscled neck and haunches, and his luxurious flowing mane. The creases in Oliver's coat where his arms bent, each unruly lock of hair that pushed out from underneath his hat, the strong cut of his jaw line, the smile in his eyes when he returned her look.

A bird in the tree high above them flitted away in a rush, causing the tiniest avalanche of snow to fall from the branch it had vacated. The snow tumbled down, growing lighter as it neared the ground and spreading into a sparkling mist that blanketed them in shimmering cold.

"Oh!" Posie exclaimed when the floating crystals touched her nose.

Oliver laughed, his smile crinkling the corners of his eyes. Neptune stamped his hooves and Honeycomb shifted underneath Posie.

Oliver eyed the horses. "They're getting antsy."

"Why?"

He glanced around at the mystical scene. "The cold. The snow." He grinned at her. "And they know what's coming?"

"What's coming?"

"The race."

"The race?" Posie's stomach cinched with nerves. "What race?"

"Only if you're comfortable," Oliver reassured her. He raised his hand and pointed down the path where it seemed to disappear into glowing white light. "To the edge of the forest and up to the top of the hill." He looked back at her, all seriousness. "But if you don't feel confident enough on Honeycomb to do that, we can hold our pace."

A thrilling whisper of delight at the idea of riding a galloping Honeycomb through the frozen wonderland expanded in her chest and soon overtook the nerves that had tightened her stomach. It was like her father used to say, *Nerves are just excitement with the brakes on.*

Too breathless to speak, Posie nodded.

Oliver grinned, eyes twinkling with fun, then hesitated. Holding back his pleasure at her response, he double checked. "Are you sure?"

Afraid that if she thought about it too long, she might back down, Posie gave him a second nod and gripped the reins. Honeycomb responded to her energy, perking her ears up and snorting.

Oliver was all smiles. "All right, we'll do it. On the count of three. One–"

Posie couldn't wait. Her whole body was ready for flight. She leaned forward slightly and pushed her heels into Honeycomb's sides. "C'mon, girl, let's go," she said under her breath. The horse's ears flicked back at the sound, instantly understanding. Honeycomb's whole body tensed then shot forward leaving Oliver's countdown in its wake.

The brakes were off. Posie was flying.

Instinctively bending forward so she would stay on the running horse, Posie took a handful of Honeycomb's mane into her hands along with the reins and held on for dear life. The closer they got to the bright white light at the end of the forest path, the faster Honeycomb ran.

Cold air turned to icy wind on her cheeks as snow sprayed up and around them. A shout from Oliver and Hagrid's barking came to her from a distance. The sound that surrounded her and her alone was the heavy rhythm of Honeycomb's breath as she ran and the muffled pounding of her hooves in the snow below.

The beat of Honeycomb's hooves reverberated up through the horse's body and into hers. The beautiful buckskin's massive frame moved strong and swift, and all Posie could do was hope she wouldn't fall off onto the cold ground that was passing by in a blur.

Another sound came to her. Another pounding beat on her left. A huge black form moved into her peripheral vision. Neptune, with Oliver on his back. They were gaining on them.

Honeycomb sensed Neptune's presence and produced a fresh burst of speed to keep ahead. Posie almost squealed, but was too overcome with fear and excitement to make any sound. She held tighter onto the piece of Honeycomb's mane in her hand and concentrated on leaning forward and staying in the saddle, trusting that the horse knew what she was doing.

They all burst out of the enchanted forest of Long Point into a glaring white winterscape. A cloud of white crystals came with them. The snow they had disturbed from its resting place billowed out in a great gust, propelled by the force of the wind the horses had created with their speed.

Posie didn't have time to look around and figure out where they were going. Honeycomb knew. She surged ahead of Neptune, jarring Posie's precarious seat on her saddle with each heaving lurch she made upward on the hill.

Posie could only hold on, heart racing in her chest, each frozen breath burning her nose and throat. She squinted into the sunshine that cut mercilessly through thin cold air then bounced back up off the surrounding drifts snow, further blinding her as Honeycomb ran the race.

Posie had no idea how fast horses could run, but she would not have been surprised if once they reached the top of the hill Honeycomb straight up into the air, flying into the sky like one of Santa's reindeer. She gripped the horse's neck with her arms and squeezed her legs tight against her sides in anticipation.

Then, as suddenly as it began, it stopped.

Honeycomb's forward trajectory slowed and leveled out. Posie straightened in her saddle and looked around just in time to turn and see Oliver pull Neptune to a full stop next to her.

"What in the hell were you doing?!" Oliver practically flew off of Neptune's back, holding onto his reins with one hand and grabbing Honeycomb's reins right beneath her bit with the other.

Posie was out of breath, but what breath she did have was being used up as laughter. She looked around again, seeing that they were at the top of a hill and assuming it was the hill Oliver had mentioned.

She slid off of Honeycomb, still laughing. Unable to stop laughing, in fact. Her legs were like jelly as she hit the ground, which for some reason made her laugh harder.

She gathered herself enough to look up at Oliver and answer, "Winning?"

He glared down at her, anger making him seem taller than usual. Sexier, too, which made Posie giggle again. She clamped her mouth shut, not wanting to laugh at his obvious concern for the horses' well being.

She patted Honeycomb's neck to show that she cared, too, but also because her legs were still a little unpredictable and she needed something to lean on. "I'm sorry, I should have thought it might have been dangerous for them to run that fast in the snow. I forgot about Neptune's leg. In my defense, you did say it was a race."

He stared at her for a moment, words failing. Then he cast his glare towards the ground, shaking his head and muttering something Posie couldn't hear.

Regret seeped into her elation and she looked worriedly at Honeycomb then Neptune's front leg. "Is she really not supposed to run that fast?"

Oliver coughed out a laugh and lifted his eyes to hers. In a clear hard tone, he said, "It wasn't Honeycomb I was worried about."

Grief for Neptune's wounded leg washed away what was left of the high she had felt after flying through the snow on Honeycomb's back. She moved next to Oliver to be closer to Neptune and patted the huge stallion's neck.

"I'm so sorry! I forgot all about his leg. Will he be all right?"

Oliver stiffened, letting the reins of both horses slip from his hands. Now calm, they stayed put. Oliver could not. He stepped away from her then turned abruptly, looked at her with fierce intensity and took a step towards her, then turned away again and took two steps before stopping.

Even with his back facing her, it was obvious he was struggling to contain his emotions. Regret filled her heart. She should have reined Honeycomb in and slowed her down. Her wild escapade had ruined their morning.

She wanted to apologize, turn the clock back and make it right. But she needed to look him in the eye to do that.

"Oliver?"

"Yes?" His voice cracked. He didn't turn around.

"I had no intention of injuring the horses."

Oliver dropped his head and looked at the ground in front of him. She could hear his deep chuckle and see it in the shake of his shoulders. He raised his head and dropped it back to look up at the sky, letting out a deep sigh.

When he turned around and looked at her, Posie's heart stopped.

The fierceness in his eyes was still there, but it wasn't anger or disappointment. It was desire. A longing so strong and clear there was no mistaking it or explaining it away as something else.

Her heart started beating again. Double time.

Oliver erased the distance between them with one determined stride and stood in directly in front of her only inches away, his breath shallow and fast. "It's you I was worried about. You, Posie."

He searched her eyes for a response, but she could give none. She was speechless. Breathless. Weightless as a snowflake floating in the freezing cold air.

Posie swallowed. "Oliver..." Without thought, her body moved into his.

Oliver touched her cheek with his leather gloved hand. His eyes fell to her lips. Posie held perfectly still, anticipating.

He cupped her chin, looked up into her eyes one last time to take her soul into his, then kissed her.

His mouth was warm, almost hot in the frosty day around them. Gentle at first, then stronger, harder. Oliver Reynolds kissed her on the top of that hill like she was his one and only and they were about to be separated forever.

And she kissed him back. Eagerly. Heat and pleasure growing inside of her as he slipped his hand from her chin to the back of her neck and pushed his body into hers, drinking her in.

When the kiss ended they did not separate, but remained holding fast to one another. Holding on for dear life.

Oliver touched his forehead to hers, his eyes dancing, short of breath. Posie laughed lightly, unable to look away from his beautiful expressive eyes.

She couldn't believe what was happening. Was she falling for this man? Was he falling for her? Emotions had risen so fast and strong in her, she couldn't wrap her mind around them. It was all like a fairy tale, a dream she might have had when she was a girl, but would never believed might come true.

"You're so beautiful," he whispered hoarsely.

Posie closed her eyes, letting the sensations of the moment sink in. She had forgotten about everything except Oliver. The cold. The horses. Hagrid's barking in the distance.

At the same moment, she and Oliver paused. Listening.

There was a change in Hagrid's bark. It was louder, sharper...closer.

They both turned at the sound and saw what he was barking at.

A group of riders came fast up the hill and stopped next to them. Posie and Oliver had been so wrapped up in each other they hadn't seen them.

The horses and their mounts kicked up snow as they stopped, the reins jingling, the horses snorting, the faces of the riders only a blur in Posie's surprise and confusion. Several people were nobody she had ever seen before, but one face at the front of the group stood out. Mainly because it was red and its eyes bulged angrily.

Oliver's grandfather, Henry Reynolds.

The next two faces she managed to recognize in the commotion were Georgina and R.C.

"Posie!" Georgina exclaimed, her mouth rounded the 'O' with utter surprise.

Posie's stomach dropped. All of the thrilling joy of a few seconds before fizzled away instantly. There was no excuse for what she'd done. Abandoning her post making ginger-bread Paris, riding around on Long Point's horses with Georgina's nephew like she belonged there, kissing him.

Had Georgina seen them kissing? She was about to lose her job and, because of that, her business and her home. She felt sick.

As Posie was trying to think of something, anything, to say in defense of herself, Grandfather Reynolds took center stage.

"What are doing, Oliver?" The old man hissed the question in a hot whisper, even though everyone present could certainly hear him.

Oliver took a step away from Posie, letting his hand slip from her waist where they had both forgotten it was. He cleared his throat, but didn't look away from his grandfather. "We were on a ride."

Grandfather Reynolds scoffed, a fleck of spittle flew out of his mouth. He leaned forward on his saddle, the leather made a creaking sound. "No, boy, that's not what I meant. What are you doing with *her*?"

All eyes turned to Posie. She wished she could melt into the snow.

"Father, is this absolutely necessary?" R.C. said, seemingly aware Posie was mortified. She didn't have the nerve to look at Georgina for her reaction.

Grandfather Reynolds waved his son's comment away and gestured at the four other riders who Posie didn't recognize at all. "Oliver, you remember Mr. Thornburg, Mr. And Mrs. Ellison, and Mr. Griffin, don't you? They're here for the week to spend the holidays with us. But you would have known that if you had been at the meeting yesterday."

Oliver nodded at his grandfather's friends. "Hello, everyone. It's nice to see you again. My apologies for missing the meeting."

Posie felt a twinge of guilt. He had been busy with her and gingerbread Paris all day.

"I thought you were too ill to attend the meeting. Or at

least that's what you led us to believe." Grandfather Reynolds put his hand on his heart and feigned concern for his grandson before a shadow fell across his face. He dropped his hand, a hostile glint in his eyes. "Imagine my surprise when we go out for a nice morning ride and find you, up to your old tricks again. Galavanting around the countryside, not a care in the world. Seducing a – a servant!"

There was a gasp. Posie was sure it came from Georgina, but she was still unable to look at the woman. The sick feeling in her stomach roiled at the harsh call out, but pride pricked at her spine. He had done nothing but try to put her down since she had arrived at Long Point. Anger pumped through her veins. Since nobody seemed capable of interrupting the old geezer's embarrassing tirade, she had no choice.

Posie jutted her chin out and gave Grandfather Reynolds the coolest, meanest stare she could muster. "I'm not a *servant*. I'm a pastry chef."

"Don't tell me what you are, girl. I already know. I know a gold digger when I see one." He spat the words at her from atop his horse then turned his scorn toward his grandson. "And this one, he'll be the ruin of everything I've built."

"That's enough!" Oliver stepped in between Posie and his grandfather.

She didn't know what happened next, because she didn't stick around to find out. With Oliver blocking her view of the old man she had a moment to glance around. Seeing Honeycomb's reins dangling free only inches away, she realized she had a chance and she took it.

Posie grabbed Honeycomb's reins, moved to the horse's side, and climbed up into the saddle. Without another word to Oliver, Georgina, or the horrible Henry Reynolds, she turned Honeycomb downhill and rode quickly back to the stables. Never turning around to see if Oliver or anyone else was coming after her.

"Ay, there, Miss, how was your ride?" Finn's easy smile dropped away the moment he saw Posie's expression. He took hold of Honeycomb's reins so she could dismount, then he glanced around looking for Oliver. "Is everything all right?"

She managed a stiff smile. "Everything's fine. I need to get back to finish the gingerbread city."

"I understand." He gave her a tip of his hat. "I'll be looking forward to seeing that when you're done. Miss Cleo can't stop talking it up."

Posie thanked him and made her way out the stable doors. She hurried down the path that led to the formal gardens outside the big house. It was a path familiar to her now. She had taken it several times. Just being on it reminded her of Oliver.

Everything about Long Point reminded her of Oliver.

Tears stung her eyes. "No, no, no," she muttered, wiping them quickly away with the back of her gloved hand. "You are not going to cry over this. You are going to go back inside and finish Paris and then get the heck out of this place."

How had she gotten into this mess? One minute she was mixing up royal icing and getting her job done, the next she was making out with Oliver Reynolds on top of a snow covered hill and being discovered by his whole dang family and their one percent posse.

She threw her head back and growled at the sky. "Posie, why do you always get so off track?"

"Posie! Wait!" Oliver's voice came from somewhere behind her.

She did not turn around. She was at the entrance to the formal gardens. If she quickened her step, perhaps she could make it to the door before Oliver reached her. Then, surrounded by the other staff members and all of the work she had to do, she could ignore him completely.

Her heart was pounding, and not just from the exertion of her walk. Fear had replaced the anger pulsing through her veins. The kind of fear that didn't come from nightmares. The kind that came from knowing everything good and loving in life could, and did, disappear in the blink of an eye. Every time.

Posie couldn't allow herself to fall for Oliver Reynolds. He didn't know what he wanted and he wasn't his own man, really. He was quite obviously under the thumb of his powerful and wealthy family, living a life that she had no business being a part of.

She blinked back more hot tears.

But in truth it wasn't all him. She couldn't allow herself the luxury of falling for anyone. Ever.

"Posie, please stop," Oliver said, grabbing her arm.

She whirled around, surprised that he had caught up with her so quickly. Out of breath, disheveled from running, he pleaded, "Please stop."

She did. But not without attitude. Pursing her lips together she waited, cold and annoyed.

"Thank you, thank you," he repeated as he bent over and put his hands on his knees, trying to catch his breath. "Hold on...just one minute...please."

Posie couldn't wait. She needed to know. "What did your grandfather mean when he said you were up to your old tricks again?"

Oliver looked up, still taking in deep breaths, and shook his head in denial. "It's not what it sounds like."

"Not what it sounds like? I'll tell you what I think it sounds like. It sounds like you do this all the time! Lurk around until some unsuspecting new employee falls into your...your trap."

Oliver straightened, still out of breath, but taking offense. "My trap? I don't have a trap."

"Oh, you don't?"

"And, for the record, I don't *lurk*."

Posie crossed her arms in front of her chest and gave him a smirk. "I don't know. You're kind of lurky."

Oliver opened his mouth to argue. When he couldn't think of an answer, he let out an incredulous laugh. Posie took the opportunity to turn around and start walking again.

"Wait, wait, wait," he begged, bounding around her and standing in her way. He looked into her eyes, his face softening. "That's not what happened. It's not what happens at all." He waited for her to respond. When she didn't he rubbed his hand roughly along the back of his neck and shook his head in frustration. "That's not what it's like."

Posie couldn't take it anymore. With every move he made and every word that came out of his mouth, she was falling harder and harder for him. This had to stop.

"Then what is it? Explain it to me. Because I've just been embarrassed and insulted and...and I'm having feelings. Real feelings, Oliver...and I'm scared."

The anxiety and confusion left his eyes, making room for a flicker of hope. "You're having feelings?"

"That's not the point." She was angry again. Better to stay angry than start crying. "I want you to explain what's going on."

"Okay, okay," Oliver agreed quickly, putting his hands on her shoulders and bending down slightly so he was looking directly into her eyes. "Firstly, my grandfather shouldn't have said those things to you. He had no right and I apologize."

He raised one eyebrow to ask if she accepted his apology. Posie shrugged half-heartedly.

Oliver kept on, "All right, that will have to do. Now, what he was referring to was one time." He held up his index finger to emphasize his point. "*One time* several years ago when I, uh, *dated* a girl, a young woman I mean, who was working in the kitchen. It was just one time. I swear." He cocked his head to see if she believed him or not. She nodded her acceptance of this explanation, though it was a reluctant nod.

"Okay, good." He relaxed a little and straightened up. His hands returned to his sides where he smoothed the front of his coat before he shoved his hands into his pockets, broke eye contact with her and looked at the ground. "There's something else you should probably know."

"Something else?"

He raised his eyes to hers and she recognized the pain and loneliness she had previously seen in him. Her heart squeezed once more, her anger melting away as he spoke.

"I, um, I have a problem being around people. A lot of people. Most people, really."

That wasn't what she had expected to hear. It didn't sound like much to confess. A lot of people were introverts. She supposed the guy who lived in a carriage house on a country estate and worked on clocks all day long would probably fall into that category.

Seeing that she hadn't been put off, he continued, "And I have a problem...leaving."

"Leaving? What, relationships?"

He shook his head 'no' and glanced around at their surroundings. When he looked back at her, his eyes were full of shame. "Leaving here. Leaving Long Point. I, um, I'm afraid to go out into the world...like a normal person."

Her thoughts froze. Oliver watched her steadily, waiting for a response. She nodded slowly, pretending that she wasn't surprised at all, that this was the kind of thing she encountered nearly every day of her life.

She wanted to clarify. "You don't ever leave Long Point?"

"Yes, I have rather acute agoraphobia. Well, it's not that

cute really." He laughed nervously then cleared his throat. "I'm prone to having panic attacks in crowds or in public. Ever since I was a little boy."

The thought of a young orphaned Oliver with big round glasses hiding in the dark servant's hallway came to her mind. Posie's resolve to keep her distance from him melted a little bit.

She continued nodding slowly and scanned the formal garden and the mansion they stood beside. Thinking about the stables and the forest and the carriage house where he spent most of his time, she finally looked back at him with an amused smile.

"I suppose if you're gonna have that problem, Long Point isn't a terrible place to have it?"

Oliver chuckled. "Yes, there are worse places to be stuck." He looked at her carefully. "I've been working on it. It's a lot better than it used to be."

"That's good." She nodded more. It was too much. She looked like a bobble-head doll. "Are you telling me this because you think it would make a difference about how I feel about you?"

"I hoped it wouldn't make any difference, but I'm telling you because...I guess I wanted you to know. I want to be up front about everything." He hesitated then risked a grin. "So you do have feelings for me?"

Posie winced comically and scratched her forehead like she was being forced to think too hard. The grin on Oliver's face grew slowly into a smile.

Mere minutes from their passionate kiss on the hill, Posie felt her cheeks and lips flush pink as Oliver moved closer. She wasn't sure how a man could be so vulnerable and masculine at the same time, but he was pulling it off. If he kissed her again, she didn't think she would have the strength to push him away.

He leaned into her, his voice a hoarse whisper, "I have another confess–"

A blood curdling scream interrupted him. They both jumped at the sound. It was coming from inside the house.

They looked at each other, alarmed, and ran together toward the house to help.

CHAPTER 16

Cleo met them at the entryway to the ballroom, her face white as snow. "It's smashed! Everything's smashed!"

"What's smashed?" Oliver asked, but Posie didn't need to hear Cleo's answer.

She knew.

Her stomach sank. Her heart rate dropped and went into super slow motion.

There were people racing around, voices talking loud and fast, but Posie's senses were dull to everything and everyone. It was all she could do to move her body across the ballroom floor, around the giant Christmas tree, and in front of the banquet table where, the last time she checked, a beautiful gingerbread Paris had stood.

No more.

Gingerbread Paris was in ruins.

The Parisian apartments, shops and Christmas market were merely mounds of crumbles in the streets. The Pont Alexandre III bridge had collapsed. The Arc de Triomphe was cracked and laying on its front. The Moulin Rouge's windmill had been torn off and the Eiffel Tower had toppled completely over.

And Notre Dame? Notre Dame was totally gone. Obliterated. Nowhere to be seen.

Posie stared in horror at the scene. Who would do this? Why?

The sound of sobbing brought her out of the fog of shock. She turned to see Georgina, still in her riding clothes, her hands covering her face, her shoulders shaking. Posie knew without asking that it was Georgina who screamed.

Slowly, carefully, Posie moved next to her client and put her hand on her shoulder. "What happened?"

Georgina jerked, yanking her hands down and turning on Posie like she was about to cuss her out. Not that Posie could blame the woman, there were a lot of things she had done just that morning that Georgina might be mad about.

Recognition registered in her eyes and Georgina's anger contorted into grief. "Oh, Posie, he's ruined everything!" She collapsed into Posie's arms.

"Who's ruined everything?" Once again, she instinctively knew the answer to her own question.

"G-g-grandfather Reynolds!" Georgina wailed into Posie's shoulder.

Anger boiled hot inside Posie's chest. What kind of psychological issues did Oliver's grandfather have, exactly? Raging around his estate, siccing vicious dogs on people, degrading employees in front of guests, bashing up gingerbread Christmas desserts like a loony old Grinch.

"This is crazy," Posie muttered under her breath.

"What did you say?" Georgina pulled away, wiping her eyes and nose on the sleeve of her riding jacket.

"Why would he do this?" Posie asked.

Georgina realized Oliver and Cleo were standing behind Posie. She turned to them and spread her arms out wide.

"You two! I'm so glad to see you together at this terrible time."

Oliver and Cleo exchanged an uncomfortable look. Oliver stepped forward and gave his aunt a cautious hug. He kept his eyes trained on Posie as he spoke, "I'm so sorry, do you know how this happened?"

"I do!" Georgina stepped away from him and swung her arms about wildly as she told her story. "I came by this morning to check on Paris and it looked absolutely marvelous." She reached out and squeezed Posie's arm, offering her a shaky smile before she continued, "Then just now, after the ride..." Georgina's eyes clouded and her gaze flicked to Posie then Oliver before landing pitifully on Cleo.

Posie stiffened, hoping Georgina was not about to reveal the fact that she and Oliver had been caught kissing. She glanced at Oliver who gave her a sheepish smile. She immediately averted her eyes away from him. Seeking a different object to look at, she scanned the room, taking note of staff members who were milling around. Rafael, Junior, a few of the maids, even Thomas the chauffeur seemed to be hanging about to see what they needed to do, if anything.

Thank goodness Margaret was nowhere to be seen. Yet.

"What happened after your ride?" Cleo asked, clueless to Posie and Oliver's discomfort.

"I came in here and – and –" Georgina covered her mouth with one shaking hand, waving her other hand in the direction of gingerbread Paris, which looked like it had been destroyed by an earthquake or tornado or other such natural disaster. "I saw this!"

"And you think Grandfather did this?" Oliver sounded skeptical.

Georgina turned narrowed eyes on him, which Posie felt were justified. "Of course I do. Who else would do something like this? He's been so adamant about the dessert being unnecessary, not important for his business partners or whatever deal he's putting together." Georgina scoffed. "As if he knows anything about entertaining. Do you know how much business gets done at a really good party?"

None of them knew.

"A lot, I can tell you. Just ask R.C." Georgina said with conviction.

Oliver pondered the ruined gingerbread city. "That may be true, but I just don't see Grandfather doing this."

"You don't?" Posie asked, a little put out that Oliver was defending his awful grandfather.

"Don't get me wrong, my grandfather is capable of a lot of things. But, honestly, I don't think he cares enough about decorations or desserts to go to this length to ruin it."

All of them stared morosely at the piles of smashed gingerbread.

Oliver continued thinking out loud, "I mean, he's more the foreclose on your family home or steal your business out from under your nose kind of guy, really."

Georgina's eyes welled up with fresh tears. She hadn't been listening to Oliver at all, just ruminating in her own thoughts. "Poor R.C., he's going to be gutted just like me. Everything completely ruined and two days before our big party...and our *anniversary*."

Posie put her arm around Georgina's shoulder, which were shaking with sobs again. Behind the older woman's back Posie gave Oliver and Cleo a despairing look. Then, with a confidence she didn't feel, she said, "Don't worry, Georgina, it's going to be fine. I promise. I can fix this."

"I CANNOT FIX THIS! Everything's ruined!" Posie lamented into her cell phone.

She had come to her room to change out of her riding clothes and call Bella, hoping for some advice or at least a friendly shoulder to cry on.

"Don't say that, Posie. You can fix anything. You're brilliant." Bella was holding up her end of the bargain, but Posie wasn't quite biting yet.

She was on her back on the bed, staring up at the ceiling, wishing she had never taken this job and never showed her face at Long Point. She pinched the bridge of her nose and let out a heavy sigh. "I don't know about that."

"You have two days until the party, right?"

"Yes, two days."

"And you have your backup pieces, right?" Bella knew how Posie worked, how most bakers who created large decorative desserts worked. There was almost always a backup.

Posie nodded. "That's true." She heard Bella talking to someone on her end.

A moment later, Mason's confident voice came on the phone. "Posie, you there?"

"Yes, I'm here."

"You're a genius. I've seen you work miracles with a little flour and sugar. You can do this!"

"Thank you, Mason. I appreciate the pep talk."

"It's not just a pep talk. It's the truth." Mason insisted. Bella's muffled voice said something to him. "Right! I didn't even think of that. Posie?"

"Yes, Mason."

"Bella wants me to remind you that it's Christmas."

Posie allowed a small smile. "I know."

"Yeah, but think about it. There's a kind of special magic at Christmas. Things tend to work out."

"You're right."

"We're sorry you're not here right now. It's not the same

without you around at Christmas." Mason really was the sweetest guy.

Posie sighed, the weight of her problems compounded by the time of year. "I'm sorry I'm not there, too, that's for sure."

"We'll see you when you get back. Here's Bella."

Posie fully appreciated the love and encouragement of her friends, but her mind was riddled with the other problem they knew nothing about. Oliver.

What had she been thinking riding around the countryside with the heir to Long Point when she should have been in the ballroom watching over her gingerbread city?

Besides, it wasn't as if Oliver was looking for someone like her. Their lives were so completely different, they would never fit together. He had more money than she could comprehend and a weird controlling uber rich family to go with it.

She was more of a scrappy loner. Always had been. Posie Miller from New York City who lived in an overpriced 400 square foot studio apartment and ran a bakery that was unlikely to survive the next year. She made fancy cakes for rich women and still couldn't make ends meet.

The whole thing was a bad idea from the beginning.

"Nothing else is going on?" Bella asked.

Posie realized she had tuned her out. "What else would be going on?"

"I don't know. You don't usually panic over pastry problems. Is there something else? Have you had a chance to fit in a little down time? Gotten enough sleep? Are you having problems with Georgina or anyone else?"

The kiss on the hill came back suddenly. The thrilling rush of it then the crashing humiliation of being discovered. Posie had to swallow her feelings in order to answer, "Maybe, but I've taken a little time off...here and there."

Bella sensed something was up. "Really? When? What did you do?"

"Just this morning. I went horseback riding."

"You did?"

"Yes, they have a nice stable here. Chock full of horses that you can ride. They just saddle them up and you take them out for a spin. You can pick your color they have so many." Posie cringed. She was talking too much.

Bella paused. "You sound funny."

Posie tried to sound normal. "No I don't. I don't sound funny at all. I sound perfectly fine."

"Ah, you see, even that sounded funny. The way you said it."

"I didn't say anything funny."

Posie could almost hear Bella's brain clicking. They had been friends a while, it wouldn't surprise her if she could pick up on her romantic troubles over a phone call.

"Tell me this, is it the gingerbread that's bothering you or is there a man?"

Posie clamped her lips together. She did not want to get involved in a man discussion. She was too tired and had too much to do. She turned her head to look at the horse and sleigh clock and see how much time was left in the day for her to try and save gingerbread Paris.

"There's no man, Bella."

"You're not fibbing, are you?"

"No fibbing. It's the gingerbread. Totally the gingerbread."

Bella hesitated, but decided to accept her answer, for now. "That's good, because unlike broken hearts, broken cookies are easy to fix. You just make more!"

CHAPTER 17

Luckily, or perhaps due to a bit of Christmas magic, Posie was relieved to discover she didn't have to bake any more gingerbread to rebuild Paris. Because of her backup pieces, of course, but also the fact that some of the cookie city survived its assault.

As she cleaned up the broken crumbles she discovered that the Arc de Triomphe could be fixed, the Moulin Rouge basically only needed its windmill blades redone and reattached, and the Eiffel Tower, to her amazement, was completely unscathed. All she had to do was carefully stand it back up, anchor its base again, and touch up a few broken bits of frosting.

"That only leaves the bridge, the Parisian apartments and shops, the Christmas market, oh, and the carousel...and Notre Dame." Posie's voice trailed off as she listed everything. Maybe 'only' wasn't the right word to describe what had to be redone.

Cleo stood beside her. "I think about three trees and four lamp posts were damaged. I can redo those pretty quickly."

Posie took in a deep breath and held it for a second

before releasing it slowly. "Okay, while you do that, I'll assemble the backup pieces so they can dry overnight and we can start decorating them tomorrow morning."

"We?" Cleo looked at her hopefully.

Posie threw her arm around the younger woman's shoulders. "Yep, Cleo, you just joined my royal icing Christmas piping boot camp!"

Cleo laughed and Posie felt a little better. At least she wasn't completely alone in this tragedy. She glanced behind her, expecting Oliver to be there. He wasn't. She had noticed his absence when she returned from changing out of her riding clothes and he had yet to return.

A pang of disappointment threatened to send her spiraling back down into despair over the entire situation. She couldn't let that happen. Bella was right, all of this could be fixed and she did have some experience dealing with tight deadlines. A lot of experience, actually. With or without Oliver, she would rebuild gingerbread Paris into something just as glorious as the first rendition. Maybe even better.

Posie picked up a chunk of broken Parisian apartment and took a bite. Cleo watched her curiously. Posie grinned. "Taste testing. It's one of the perks. It's good, you should try one." She motioned for Cleo to take her own treat from the pile. "No sense letting it all go to waste."

Cleo carefully picked up one of the ruined horses from the carousel, but instead of biting into it she peered at it more closely. "This looks like it's been chewed."

Posie swallowed and inspected the edge of the horse Cleo held up for her to see. There definitely wasn't a clean break like with the piece she was eating. Cleo's gingerbread looked like something had gnawed on it.

"What is that from?" Posie wondered out loud. The first image that came to her mind was Oliver's grandfather chewing ravenously on the carousel horse. That seemed unlikely.

Cleo sucked in her breath. "Could it be a rat?"

Posie glanced around the opulent ballroom and shook her head. Her eyes fell on the big pile of gingerbread ready to be tossed out. "I doubt there are rats here, plus that's way too much destruction for a rat. Someone would have noticed a swarm of rats, wouldn't they?"

Cleo nodded. "Of course, but...what other kind of animal is around that would do such a thing?"

Posie froze. She knew exactly what other type of animal was around that might do such a thing. She knew two such animals, in fact. "A dog."

Cleo's eyes grew wide. "You think Hagrid did this?"

Posie shook her head 'no'. "Hagrid doesn't like gingerbread, and he doesn't run around the big house anyway."

"That's true. He never comes in with Oliver."

"But I know of two other dogs who cause trouble."

"The guard dogs?"

Posie nodded grimly. "The guard dogs."

"What about the guard dogs?" Oliver asked. He had entered unnoticed while they were scrutinizing the gingerbread.

Ignoring how her heart picked up its pace when she saw him, she showed him the piece of chewed gingerbread. "It looks like an animal gnawed on some of this. I think it could have been a dog, or two."

Oliver took the gingerbread out of her hand and inspected it himself. He cursed under his breath and shook his head as he turned the ruined cookie in his hand. "It sure does look like a used up dog toy."

Cleo's brow wrinkled. "How are we going to keep them from doing this again?"

Oliver's eyes shot up. He pressed his lips together,

containing his angry thoughts, but not the glint in his eyes. He forced a smile. "We'll figure it out." He took a few steps back. "If you'll excuse me, I have to attend to something. I'll be back as soon as I can." Then he turned on his heel and walked swiftly out of the ballroom, still holding the chewed up piece of gingerbread.

Posie's stomach twisted. He was going to confront his grandfather, she was almost certain of it. Anxiety over that confrontation filled her with dread on his account. It also filled her with affection for him, warming her heart that he would try to defend gingerbread Paris, her creation, even though it was bound to cause a big scene.

She turned to Cleo with renewed gusto. "All right, let's get going on this. I'll whip up a new batch of royal icing while you get going on those lamp posts and trees."

They were well into the rebuild when Oliver finally returned. Posie's heart sank when she saw his face. He looked miserable.

"How'd it go?" she asked.

He gave a curt shake of his head. "Not good."

Posie and Cleo shared a look of doom while Oliver stared gloomily at the floor. He obviously didn't want to spill the details of his encounter with Grandfather Reynolds.

Posie sighed. "Well, I guess all we can do is rebuild and hope for the best."

"I think one of us should stay in here 24/7 until the party," Oliver said, still staring at the floor.

"All night?" Cleo's eyes widened.

He nodded, finally lifting his gaze to meet Posie's. "I don't know how else to guarantee this won't happen again. My grandfather insists the dogs were in their pen this morning at sunrise and refuses to entertain any other scenario. Maybe they were and they did their damage in the middle of the night, but nobody saw it until later."

Posie shook her head 'no'. "I came through on my way to the stables before we went riding. Nothing was damaged then."

Oliver made a frustrated growling sound and shoved his hand through his hair. "He is so...so...immovable. Like a huge slippery unclimbable wall built out of gold bricks. Incapable of seeing anything other than what he wants to see."

They all stood in silent despair, pondering their predicament. It was Posie who drew them out of it. She had been in difficult situations before and at least she knew what to do with this one.

She threw back her shoulders and stood up tall. "So be it. I'll stay the night in here to keep gingerbread Paris safe." Looking between Oliver and Cleo, she shrugged and grinned. "I'm going to be working late on all of this anyway. I probably won't get any sleep either way. Besides, it's my job and my responsibility."

Oliver and Cleo vowed to take shifts so she could get some sleep and the whole plan went into motion.

Later that night, when she was done putting together all of the new structures, Posie had a change of heart. She sat down heavily in a chair next to the banquet table and let her head drop back to stare at the ceiling. Cleo had long since gone to bed so she would be fresh in the morning. Oliver was working on the Moulin Rouge windmill mechanics.

"Don't you have to let those dry until morning?" he asked.

She nodded, her eyes closing involuntarily.

Oliver put the piece of the windmill he was holding down carefully and gave her a steady look. "Why don't you go to bed?"

Posie shook her head 'no' and mumbled, "I'm all right."

"Posie." Oliver's tone made her open one eye and roll her head to the side to look at him. He gestured to the windmill pieces and the carousel, which was all put together but still needed him to insert the music box player. "I still have things to do and you don't. I'll do the graveyard shift and you go get some sleep so you can be fresh in the morning."

She didn't have the strength to argue with his logic. And there was the fact that what he said made perfect sense. Bleary eyed, Posie made her way to her room and collapsed into a deep sleep.

She woke up on her own, more rested than she had expected to feel. The clock on the side of the golden sleigh read 6:00am. Tomorrow was Christmas Eve, but she had the entire day in front of her. Without any further distractions she should be able to put her nose to the ol' grindstone and get gingerbread Paris ready in time for the party on Christmas Day.

The halls of Long Point were still quiet as she made her way to the ballroom, which was how she was able to hear voices in the ballroom as she approached the entryway. Heated voices.

She slowed her pace, gripped with anxiety. Visions of a partially reconstructed Paris utterly destroyed – again – made her flinch as what sounded like an argument grew louder. She paused just before the entrance, taking in a deep breath to calm her nerves. Closing her eyes, she whispered, "It's a giant cookie, Posie. Nothing that can't be fixed."

The voices continued. She recognized both of them. One was Oliver's. The other, Georgina's.

Shaking her arms and shoulders like a prize fighter about to enter the ring, Posie took in another deep breath and braced herself for what she was about to see. Then she stepped around the corner into the ballroom.

Oliver locked eyes with her soon after she entered. It was obvious to her that he was standing his ground against Georgina. His jaw was rigid, his eyes flashed, his whole body was held tight in opposition to whatever his aunt was saying.

And she was saying a lot.

Georgina was quite upset and letting him know it. Her voice was raised in panic, her arms flapped and flailed as she gesticulated towards gingerbread Paris, Oliver, the giant Christmas tree, and pretty much everything else in the ballroom – except Posie, she hadn't seen her yet.

Posie couldn't make out everything her client was saying, but several words traveled across the ballroom crystal clear.

Nothing…Impossible…Disaster…

Not super encouraging, but Posie managed to keep her cool as she approached the argument. Mainly because she could see gingerbread Paris was still intact. At least that wasn't the problem.

"There's nothing else we can do. It's the day before Christmas Eve. There's nobody else I trust who can get here in time," Georgina was practically shouting at Oliver.

Oliver switched his attention between his aunt and Posie as she neared, but his expression remained resolute. "You can't ask that of someone, Georgina. It's a ridiculous amount of work with everything else that's going on."

He had dropped the polite use of Georgina's title of 'Aunt', which Posie took as a sign of real trouble.

Finally at Georgina's side, though still unnoticed, Posie squared her shoulders, ready to address whatever catastrophe had occurred. "Good morning," she said in her calmest, pastry chef in charge voice. "What's going on?"

Georgina whirled around, her eyes wet and rimmed with red. She took urgent hold of Posie's shoulders with cool, trembling hands, her rings and bracelets clinking. "Thank goodness you're here! We have an emergency and you're the only one who can fix it."

"Georgina, that's not true–" Oliver began his argument anew, but stopped when Posie shot him a look.

If her client had a pastry related issue, Posie was the one

who needed to handle it. She was being paid for her services. Not to mention that she desperately needed to live up to Georgina's expectations to ensure that she did get paid. Besides, she was used to working with high maintenance clients.

"What is it you would like fixed?" she asked, still in her calming, confident chef zone.

"We don't have a real dessert!" Georgina exclaimed, her voice rising in pitch with each word.

Posie blinked a few times as the words sunk in. She glanced at gingerbread Paris, then at Oliver, then brought her attention back to Georgina. "A real dessert." She repeated, realizing as each moment went by what Georgina meant.

And that she was right.

In one devastating instant Posie understood her own major oversight. With the change from designer cake to gingerbread city for the party, the main dessert was, basically, inedible. Not that gingerbread Paris wasn't edible, but if people ate it during the party the entire look would be destroyed.

"We can't let people eat this gorgeous creation." Georgina's brow pinched with worry, as much as the botox allowed anyway. "And I didn't tell Rafael to plan anything."

Posie shook her head, coming out of her shock and kicking herself for neglecting her duties. "No, no, you're right, but I should have thought of that."

Oliver coughed out in disagreement. "You can't do everything." Both women looked at him. He pointed at gingerbread Paris. "You've been overwhelmed with this all week. How could you possibly be responsible for every other aspect of this party?"

The back of Posie's neck tensed and her jaw tightened. She leveled her gaze onto Oliver. "I'm the pastry chef. It's my responsibility."

He scoffed in disbelief. "She changed everything on you at the last minute. And then you had to redo the whole thing again."

She dismissed his excuses with a curt shake of her head. "I should have – I should have discussed everything with Rafael and made accommodations. It's my job."

Georgina squeezed Posie's shoulders warmly and let go. "You're an absolute wonder. I know you'll come up with something fabulous for the guests to actually eat." She turned newly bright eyes toward gingerbread Paris. "This party is going to be the talk of the season."

Oliver blustered, "Georgina, you're being ridiculous. You can't just –"

"Cleo! Darling!" Georgina ignored his protests and turned to greet her niece who had arrived unseen, as usual. "You're here just in time. Posie's going to save the day again!"

Proudly carrying a low tray holding replacement chocolate trees and lamp posts, Cleo gave Posie a puzzled look. "What needs saving now?"

CHAPTER 18

Oliver fumed as Georgina excitedly filled Cleo in on the additional work Posie would be doing.

Cleo's eyes grew round with surprise. "Dessert for 500 people?"

"It's only a little over 400," Georgina corrected, smiling conspiratorially at Cleo. "And you'll be there to help her." She looked meaningfully at Oliver. "And so will he."

Oliver glared at her.

"Won't you be there to help, Oliver?" Georgina continued, swishing her hand in the direction of the Moulin Rouge, whose windmill was turning smoothly. "You've been such a help already."

Oliver held his tongue, making his jaw clench. He answered his aunt while looking directly at Posie. "I will do whatever I can to help."

"Good, maybe you and Cleo can team up on your own so Posie can concentrate on what she needs to do." Georgina smiled again, but less genuine. More like a boss announcing the annual Christmas party was going to be a potluck instead of fine dining.

It didn't take a genius to understand Georgina's meaning. She was still pushing Oliver and Cleo together. Not that any of that mattered anymore to Posie. All of her energy was focused on not slipping into a pit of despair. She could not afford to abandon hope now. She had to get the job done by Christmas Day.

Georgina pulled Cleo away to admire her chocolate creations and Oliver took the opportunity to speak to Posie alone.

He watched her closely and spoke low enough Georgina wouldn't overhear, "You can't do this, Posie. You're barely going to get Paris done. It's too big of an ask. You're exhausted."

"Don't." Posie stopped him.

He was standing close. Much too close. His presence kept her distracted. In fact, his presence was probably one of the reasons she hadn't thought about the dessert issue to begin with. She'd spent too much time with him, riding horses, doing all kinds of things except what she was there to do.

She held his gaze and set her jaw. "I appreciate your concern, but I really don't need you to protect me from my literal job."

"You need–"

"What I need to do is finish this job. Get paid. And go home." Posie interrupted, ignoring the surprise in Oliver's eyes at her abrupt response.

Reluctant acceptance filled his eyes as they lingered on hers for a few long moments. Then he stepped away, nodding. "Whatever you think is best."

Posie hated what he said and the way that he said it. She hated what she had said and how she had said it. But none of that could be helped at the moment. She had more urgent matters to attend to.

When she sat down with Rafael in the conservatory, she

was apologetic and grateful for his kind response. Chefs were not always the most agreeable personalities, but Rafael was a gem.

"I, too, should have put more thought into this, Posie. I think we could have used a good meeting of the minds this past week. Perhaps we could have avoided this dilemma." He smiled warmly.

Relieved, she tried to reassure him, "I don't want you or your staff to worry about anything. I'll make the additional dessert."

He furrowed his brow. "Are you certain you can complete Paris as well?"

"Well, Cleo will help me, of course," Posie began. She ignored the doubt in Rafael's eyes. "She's gotten quite good at a few fundamentals."

"And what have you decided on for the dessert?"

Posie hesitated before answering, "Gingerbread."

Rafael lifted his eyebrows. "Really?"

"Gingerbread man cookies. We have all of the supplies. Cleo has experience with the dough. They're fairly simple to decorate." She shrugged. "Besides I think everyone at the party might be craving gingerbread once they see gingerbread Paris."

Rafael laughed. "Indeed! Well, I still think you might benefit from having more help. I'll recruit some of the other staff who have some free time if you like."

Posie agreed and pretty soon she and Cleo had put together a small production line of gingerbread men in their allotted kitchen space. Junior had graciously offered to pitch in and soon the already bustling kitchen was transformed into a festive Christmas workshop. Savory and sweet aromas filled the air as Posie painstakingly guided Cleo through the steps of gingerbread man decoration.

They were so busy, she didn't realize Oliver had come into the kitchen until Cleo greeted him.

"Look, Oliver! Do you like it?" Cleo proudly held up a completed gingerbread man, whose piped edges had little to no wobbly bits at all.

"That looks good, Cleo." He smiled encouragingly then rubbed his hands together. "What can I do to help?"

Before Posie could answer, something in the easy camaraderie of the kitchen shifted. She turned to the kitchen entrance to see what the rest of the staff were looking at.

Georgina.

Breezing into the kitchen as if she spent every morning there making toast and coffee, the lady of the house came directly to the gingerbread man decorating station.

"How is it going? Oh, my goodness! These are adorable!" She picked up one of Cleo's recently decorated cookies and sat down on an empty stool to inspect it.

"I decorated that one," Cleo told her, beaming.

"It's beautiful, just beautiful," Georgina beamed back.

Posie kept quiet, pretending it was taking all of her concentration to pipe little eyes and buttons on the gingerbread men, but all the while hoping against hope Georgina wasn't going to have another epiphany. Oliver also said nothing, probably wondering the same thing, but cognizant that he had said enough on the subject already.

Georgina gasped, putting her hand on her heart. "I have an idea!"

Posie closed her eyes and controlled a groan. What now?

"I want to try." Georgina's eyes shone with excitement.

Momentarily confused, Posie stared mutely at her client.

Cleo stepped in to help. "You want to decorate a cookie?"

Georgina nodded with enthusiasm. "It looks so fun."

Cleo looked at Posie for permission. Relieved at the simple request, Posie nodded, adding, "Of course. What if

Cleo taught you? She can show you everything she's learned."

Pleased that Georgina would be kept busy for a while, and apparently had no other ulterior motive than to have a little festive fun, Posie turned back to decorating.

"Oliver, why don't you join us?" Georgina suggested, gesturing to the empty stool next to Cleo.

Posie's stomach clenched. There was the ulterior motive. Still, she didn't respond, even when Oliver tried to catch her eye before reluctantly joining Cleo and his matchmaker aunt.

Sensing the underlying tension, Cleo tried to lighten the mood. "Posie says we can add whatever we want to the normal three buttons. So you can make whatever kind of gingerbread man you like." She smiled at Oliver. "A little creative Christmas fun."

With a sly smile, Georgina added, "And it's a great way for you two to spend some time together."

Posie's tight stomach turned over, sending a sickening wave through her body. This was all becoming unbearable. The pressure of the job ahead, Georgina being, well, *Georgina*, and the feelings she had for Oliver, a man who lived in a world where she could never fit in, were too much.

She put down her piping bag. "We'll run out of cookies to decorate with all of you helping. I'll get some more in the oven."

She felt better at the mixer. Measuring the ingredients, watching them churn together, the sound drowning out everything around her, the spicy scent, all of it gave her something to think of other than her actual reality. When the dough was done she turned the mixer off, unfortunately, just in time to listen in.

"I must say, Oliver, you and Cleo make a great team," Georgina cooed.

Posie flipped the mixer back on angrily, daring to glance at

Oliver for his reaction. He was bent over a gingerbread man, piping bag in hand, silent and frowning, seemingly unwilling to engage in further banter. She took some comfort in that, but only some.

She turned the mixer off once more and immediately heard Margaret's biting tone.

"I hope you have everything in order, Miss Miller," the formidable housekeeper swept through the kitchen. When she realized who was sitting at the counter decorating gingerbread men, she stopped short. "Mrs. Reynolds, Mr. Oliver..." her voice trailed off as she cast a critical eye on the scene. She flicked a scathing look at Posie before asking Georgina, "You're decorating, ma'am?"

Georgina, who possessed a host of her own haughty and scathing looks, leveled one of them on Margaret. "What have I told you about calling me 'ma'am', Margaret?"

Margaret's lips tightened even more than normal. "Sorry, ma'am – I mean, Mrs. Reynolds."

Georgina waved her hand, dismissing the incident like a queen who had chosen to overlook a dire offense. "Now, how are preparations for the party going? Is everything on schedule?"

Relieved to change the subject, Margaret answered, "Yes. Everything is on schedule. There will be no mistakes. Your Christmas Day party will be flawless."

"Good." Georgina gave no more praise. Posie sensed she liked Margaret about as much as everyone else.

Margaret stiffened under the lady of the house's cool response. She clasped her hands together tightly and nodded in short jerks. "Yes, none of that terrible business with the dogs will happen again, I assure you."

All of them paused and turned to the housekeeper. Oliver put down his piping bag and sat up straight.

Cleo couldn't help but blurt out, "You mean the guard dogs did it?"

"Did what?" Georgina wanted to know.

Margaret wrung her hands, but remained steadfastly stiff as she responded, "I believe it was Thor and Diesel who destroyed the gingerbread city the other day."

Georgina blinked a few times as the news sunk in. "Thor and Diesel ate Paris? It wasn't Grandfather Reynolds who tore it apart?"

Margaret looked shocked. "No, of course not. Why would Henry—I mean Mr. Reynolds—do something like that? No, the dogs were out and were seen near the ballroom that morning."

Oliver cursed under his breath. Posie felt vindicated that she had been right, but the tension emanating from the others in the room was palpable.

Oliver's simmering frustration boiled over. He stood abruptly. "Why does Grandfather insist on keeping those beasts?"

Flustered at the trouble her confession had caused, Margaret tried to reassure him. "I've since made sure they are secure, Mr. Oliver. They won't get out again."

Georgina remained flabbergasted. "You were right, Oliver. He didn't do it."

Oliver tapped his index finger on the counter next to the gingerbread man he had just decorated. "But he did do it. By keeping those dangerous animals around in the first place and not having them properly looked after."

Margaret bristled. "I always follow Mr. Reynold's instructions with the dogs. No harm was intended."

Oliver shook his head in disgust and stormed off. Posie knew he was going to confront his grandfather again. She also knew where that conversation would likely lead. To her. To the fact that Grandfather Reynolds thought she was a gold digger.

The mounting chaos surrounding her and gingerbread Paris was becoming more taxing. She needed things to go well and move quickly. Her lonely little apartment and struggling bakery seemed a thousand miles away at the moment, but they were also growing more and more appealing compared to the mess at Long Point.

Posie pressed her forehead with the back of her hand. A headache was threatening to take over and she couldn't have that. An idea popped into her head. Probably a fight or flight reaction, but it made her feel strong enough to go on. She would make arrangements to go home right after the Christmas party instead of the morning after. What did she have to stick around for here anyway? Everything she touched seemed to fall apart.

Cleo had joined her at the mixer. She leaned in and asked, "Do you think Oliver will be okay?"

Posie, her gaze focused on the task before her, replied, "He'll handle it. Right now we need to finish these gingerbread men so I can finish gingerbread Paris."

Cleo sensed Posie's exhaustion. "Tomorrow's Christmas Eve. Do you really think we can get everything done?"

Posie managed a brave smile. "We're going to have to hope for a little bit of Christmas magic to help, that's all."

CHAPTER 19

Christmas Eve arrived with a sense of urgency, and the grand estate buzzed with excitement. The entire staff gathered to lend a hand in the festive preparations and still managed to offer Posie additional help, as Rafael had promised.

Not only the kitchen staff, but a few of the maids, one of the groundskeepers, Thomas the chauffeur, and even Finn arrived to assist in the baking and decorating of gingerbread men. They needed 1200 cookies total, in Posie's opinion. That allowed for three per guest at the party. And 1200 gingerbread men took an army to bake.

"I'm afraid I've got too heavy a hand for this fine work," Finn told Posie and Cleo as he watched Cleo deftly outlining one of the gingerbread men with white icing. "But I'm happy to lift and carry or mop up after any messes along the way."

"Thank you, Finn." Posie smiled in gratitude, but her smile was lost on the handsome stable manager. He could barely take his eyes off of Cleo. In return, Cleo smiled coyly and, to Posie's pleasant surprise, seemed to bloom under his attention.

The lively banter between the two unlikely love birds added an extra layer of fun to the bustling atmosphere. However, Posie's heart sank a little bit every time she thought about Oliver's absence. She hadn't seen him since he stormed off to confront his grandfather and concern for him lingered in her mind as she worked.

Still, she scarcely had a moment to consider Oliver or Grandfather Reynolds. Gingerbread Paris remained incomplete in the ballroom and there was no extra help at Long Point who could finish it except her.

She whipped up a fresh batch of royal icing and filled several piping bags before telling Cleo, "I think you've got everything under control here, I'm going to finish Paris. I'll be in the ballroom if you need me."

Alarm registered on Cleo's face. "Are you sure?"

Posie gave her an encouraging pat on the back. "Absolutely! Look at you, you're like an old pro. You've got this."

Finn chimed in, "I'll be at your beck and call, too, Miss Cleo. Anything you need, just ask."

With gingerbread man production under Cleo's competent, if slightly insecure, management, Posie made her way to the ballroom. After the busy early morning she was looking forward to the peace and quiet of the ballroom so she could bury herself in piping decorations and hopefully stop wondering where Oliver had disappeared to.

Gingerbread Paris provided ample opportunity to lose herself in her work, but there was no peace and quiet to be had at all. The ballroom was humming with its own energy. More greenery strung with lights was being added, the banquet tables near hers, which had previously been empty, were being dressed to serve food, and florists were delivering enormous fresh flower and pine bouquets to embellish the existing Christmas decorations. One of the maids had a cart laden with beautifully wrapped Christmas gifts, which she was placing carefully under the tree, and equipment for a small orchestra was being set up in one corner of the room.

The mood was bright and the spirit of Christmas permeated every corner. Pride swelled in Posie's heart as she moved closer to gingerbread Paris. Even though it wasn't finished, it still drew attention with its special mix of elegance and fun. People were pausing in their duties to stop and admire the cookie city and Posie was both relieved and pleased.

Thomas the chauffeur was one of those people. As Posie approached he caught her eye. "You really have pulled off a miracle with this."

"Well, I'm not quite done with it yet," she answered.

Thomas chuckled and gave her a knowing look. "I have faith in you, Miss. You've got that jingle bell spirit, I can see it in your eyes."

Posie had to laugh. "Jingle bell spirit? I've never heard of that before."

Thomas nodded in mock seriousness. "Well, you've got it. I'd wager that you don't let much stop you."

"Maybe, it's probably just from growing up in the City."

Thomas nodded and chuckled again. "That might explain it."

"Thomas, I meant to ask you, if it's not too much trouble, would it be possible to get a ride to the station tomorrow. After the party?"

"You're leaving us on Christmas Day?"

She ignored the stab of misery her special request was causing in her own heart. "I need to get back as soon as possible."

"Of course, I'm sure you want to spend at least some of the holiday with your family."

She forced a smile. "Yes, exactly."

With her plans in place and no other distractions, Posie set about completing the fine pipework on her gingerbread masterpiece. She felt a little like a New York City window display as people came and went, pausing to watch her for a few minutes along the way. Still, she managed to get into the zone and work quickly, the pang of heartache over leaving Long Point, and the elusive Oliver, shrinking to the back of her mind.

"Posie, it's amazing!" Cleo exclaimed.

Posie looked up, surprised to see not only Cleo, but Finn as well, watching her work. She had no idea how much time had gone by since she came to the ballroom.

Finn let out a low whistle as he admired gingerbread Paris. "Hats off to you, Miss Posie. This is quite the looker."

Posie glanced back and forth between the two of them, picking up on a distinct difference in the way they were standing together. Closer. More comfortable. She caught a twinkle in Cleo's eye and smiled. The bashful, awkward young woman Posie had met just a few days ago was gone. She was certain something romantic had occurred in the kitchen between Cleo and the gallantly good looking Finn.

"Thank you," Posie said. Then, a little mischievously. "How is everything going in the kitchen?"

Before Cleo could answer, another voice chimed in, taking over their conversation.

"Posie, darling, we've come to save the day!" Georgina announced as she approached them. She was followed by her crew of wealthy girlfriends. Surrounded by an air of sophistication, they all seemed a little out of place in a room that wasn't quite ready for the party yet.

Posie noticed one of the women had been a rider in the group who caught her and Oliver kissing. Half of the Mr. and Mrs. Ellison Grandfather Reynolds had introduced to try and point out Oliver's neglect of the family business.

Ignoring the embarrassment that memory brought up, she put on a welcoming smile. "Save the day?"

"I had so much fun yesterday helping with the cookies," Georgina began.

Posie was pretty sure it had only been one cookie, but she didn't interrupt.

"I thought we could all help decorate the gingerbread men. Get in the Christmas spirit, you know?" Georgina looked around expectantly. As if by saying they were going to help, they were already helping. "We're going to set up in here. The kitchen is too hot."

Posie felt precious time slipping away as she tried to wrap her head around this new development. Time she desperately needed to finish gingerbread Paris.

Cleo picked up on her panic and stepped in. "We'll go get some cookies and icing and bring everything in here." She didn't even look at Finn for confirmation that he was part of the 'we' she spoke of. They were definitely an item.

"I would appreciate that," Posie said gratefully.

"Don't you worry about the gingerbread men. Cleo has everything under control. She's a fine baker," Finn reassured her.

Cleo and Finn took wonderful care of Georgina and her friends so Posie could keep working on gingerbread Paris. Cleo answered all of their questions about baking and decorating and, from what Posie overheard, the girl had absolutely been paying attention while being her assistant. Finn, on the other hand, smiled and winked and generally flirted with the socialite ladies, which kept them happy.

Posie couldn't help but notice that he saved his most sincere flattery for Cleo, which warmed her heart. The dull ache that had taken over in her chest ever since she asked Thomas to schedule her leaving was eased slightly at the knowledge that at least someone's budding holiday romance would survive into the new year.

From her vantage point at gingerbread Paris, Posie could

see that Cleo and Finn's flirtations were not going unnoticed by Georgina. She wondered if her client might give up on the idea of Cleo and Oliver, or if Finn would face the same gold digger accusations that she had experienced. Judging from the look on Georgina's face while Finn gently placed his hand on Cleo's lower back as they walked together, Posie thought Georgina might approve of him in the end.

The afternoon stretched into evening. Georgina and her friends completed their foray into baking and moved on to entertain themselves somewhere else. Cleo managed the rest of the gingerbread man production in the kitchen. The ballroom continued to be a hub of activity as everyone did their part to prep for the party.

In the midst of the organized chaos, Posie continued piping. Though her wrists and forearms ached and she felt like her skin had somehow absorbed royal icing to the point that she, herself, was sugar coated, she was thrilled. The empty spaces crying out for frosting grew smaller and smaller until, almost to her surprise, they were filled.

She was done.

Glancing around, she realized she was largely alone, save for a few people checking the sound system for the orchestra and a team shining the marble floor.

All of gingerbread Paris stood strong, proud, and graceful. The white decorations, twinkling lights, turning windmill, and working carousel playing "Dance of the Sugar Plum Fairies" brought it to life. Posie stood back, quietly admiring her handiwork. She could hardly believe the whole city was complete.

"It's really beautiful, Posie."

She whirled around to find Oliver behind her, smiling sheepishly. The urge to wrap her arms around him in celebration clashed with a flash of anger at his day long absence and she ended up simply staring up at him, confused.

He looked tired. His hair was tousled, his jeans and sport coat were wrinkled and disorderly, like he had worn them to bed, or perhaps never gone to bed at all.

"Oliver," she said, her voice was hoarse. She hadn't spoken a word to anyone in several hours as she finished gingerbread Paris. Come to think of it, she probably looked like she had been up all night as well.

"You did it." He smiled and the smile spread all the way into his eyes.

Posie nodded and let out a deep breath. "It's done."

They both started to speak at the same time then stopped, not sure what to say.

He took her by the hand and her heart flipped in her chest.

He backed up a few steps, pulling her gently with him in the direction of the Christmas tree. "I have something for you."

"For me?" She went with him, but not because he was going to give her a gift. At that moment, with his eyes shining mischievously, in the beautifully decorated ballroom, Tchaikovsky plinking away in the background, Posie probably would have gone with him anywhere.

Oliver positioned her next to the Christmas tree so they were out of the view of the others still in the room. He reached into the inside pocket of his sport coat and frowned. He tried his other pocket and became distracted. Posie watched, amused, as his search became more frantic.

"What is it?" she asked, letting her gaze wander over the lines of his jaw, his strong nose, his unruly hair. As he clumsily hunted through his pants pockets and his sport coat pocket, his glasses began to slip down his nose. In the shimmering light of the Christmas tree, his bumbling clock maker look was nearly irresistible.

"I thought I had—" he stopped suddenly, relief flooding his features. "Here it is."

Slowly, humbly, he held out his hand and offered her a small green box tied with a white ribbon. "I wanted to...I made you a..." In his desire to explain, he couldn't find the words.

"Where have you been, Oliver?" She wasn't trying to sound wounded. It just came out that way.

A little surprised at the question, Oliver had to switch gears. "Oh, I, um, well, I had to speak to grandfather. About the dogs."

"Right," Posie nodded. That had been yesterday. Did he really think she would believe he had spent all that time with his grandfather?

He took her hand again and placed the gift in it. "I wanted to give you something for Christmas. I made it...for you."

"You made me something?"

He smiled, watching with cautious excitement as she untied the white ribbon and opened the box to reveal a beautiful gold necklace with a clock pendant in the shape of a miniature horse—reminiscent of the larger version in her room.

Touched, she looked up at him, all of her frustration over not seeing him all day disappeared. "Oliver, it's beautiful. Thank you."

"Do you like it?" He pointed at the graceful head and ears of the horse. "I had a hard time getting the ears right."

"The ears are perfect. I love it, I really do."

He blushed, full on blushed, and dropped his gaze to the floor under her praise. Charmed by his reaction, all Posie wanted to do was step into his arms and let him kiss her again, just like he had kissed her on the hill.

But this wasn't the place and she wasn't completely sure it would ever be the time again, not between the two of them.

When Oliver lifted his eyes to hers, something perfect and true raced through her body. Something she never thought she would know with such certainty.

Love.

She was in love with Oliver Reynolds.

He had captured her, heart and soul.

And she was leaving tomorrow.

Posie pulled away from him, realizing suddenly that she had been moving closer with each tick of the second hand on the horse pendant. Emotion clutched at her throat, but she managed to say, "But I didn't get you anything."

His face lit up. He smiled slowly. "Yes, you did."

"Oliver!" A man's voice called out, ending their intimate moment by the Christmas tree.

Grandfather Reynolds and R.C. had stepped into the ballroom, looking for Oliver.

"I'm here." Oliver answered them as he stepped away from her with an apologetic smile. "Duty calls, I'm afraid."

Posie nodded, unable to form an answer.

Before he turned and left, Oliver gave her one last questioning look. "You'll be at the party, won't you?"

She nodded, elation and grief swirling through her core, and watched him walk away.

CHAPTER 20

Christmas morning was a cheerful affair spent with the staff in the cozy warmth of the conservatory, the heart of Long Point for those who worked there, and a beautiful place to share a delicious breakfast. Ever thoughtful of feeding the staff as well as his employers and their guests, Rafael had whipped up several pans of gooey sweet cinnamon rolls, sausage and mushroom quiche, freshly squeezed orange juice, and the hot, delicious coffee that was a staple in his kitchen.

Posie didn't just manage to keep her spirits up during breakfast, she actually had a good time. She had grown quite fond of Rafael and Junior as well as Finn and Thomas. Their good cheer on the special morning was mirrored by the rest of the staff, even Margaret, who showed up to breakfast wearing a lush red velvet bath robe and carrying a stack of Christmas cards in expensive envelopes.

"Merry Christmas, Margaret," Rafael greeted her with a twinkle in his eyes. "I see you are carrying on the tradition this year."

"Of course, Rafael, it's a Merry Christmas every year," Margaret responded in a lighter tone than Posie had ever heard her speak before. She began delivering her Christmas cards to their recipients whose names were written in beautiful script on the face of each envelope.

Finn leaned over to Posie and explained, "It's tradition every year on Christmas morning for our Margaret to relax her normal talon like grip on formality. Let her hair down a little and don the jolly red robe of the Christmas spirit."

Thomas chuckled at Posie's surprise. "And she hands out the Christmas bonuses. She's like our very own Santa Claus."

"I heard that, Thomas, and I'll thank you not to compare me to a very fat, very old man." Margaret eyed him with what was almost a smile on her face and handed him his Christmas card.

Thomas laughed and the deep merry sound brought on a round of laughter from everyone else at the table. The family-like camaraderie was a pleasant surprise for Posie on what she had expected to be a lonely Christmas day.

"And for you," Margaret said, handing Posie the last envelope.

"For me?" Posie looked at the thick envelope in her hand and, sure enough, her name was written in bold, beautiful hand.

"Merry Christmas," Margaret said.

Posie believed that she meant it, too.

Inside the envelope was an exquisite Christmas card depicting a painted image of the front of Long Point decorated for Christmas under a starry sky with the addition of Santa and his reindeer flying overhead. A 'Merry Christmas and a Joyous New Year' message from the Reynolds family was handwritten inside and signed by Grandfather Reynolds, R.C. and Georgina, and Oliver.

Posie's heart cinched at the sight of his signature on her card. A poignant reminder of their employer–employee relationship. She didn't have long to brood over it, however, because she found an unexpected surprise inside the envelope.

A check. Two checks, in fact.

One was to the name of her business for the amount she and Georgina had agreed upon and was marked 'For services rendered' in the memo. The other was filled out in her name, simply said 'Merry Christmas' in the memo section, and was for twice the amount of the first check.

Posie stared in silence at the two checks, stunned. Relief and joy rushed through her, but more powerful feelings soon rose up.

Longing. Regret. Knowing that Oliver was mostly likely celebrating Christmas morning with his family, hidden away in the most private rooms of Long Point, the rooms reserved for family and guests only. The rooms that were not meant for her, a lowly pastry chef. That knowledge dulled her initial elation from getting paid three times more than she had planned on.

Finn nudged her and asked expectantly, "Did you get a Christmas bonus, too, Miss Posie?"

"Yes, I did." Posie tried to return his enthusiastic smile. She knew the appropriate response was to feel as if she had won some kind of prize. So why did she have a sinking feeling that she had lost something dear?

She didn't see Oliver the rest of the day, spending most of it packing up her tools in the kitchen then retiring to her room to pack her clothes. Cleo came by the kitchen to ask her if she wanted to go for a Christmas morning ride, but Posie didn't have the heart. Being in the stables, riding Honeycomb, all of that sounded wonderful, but it would be laced with the grief that she was about to leave it—and Oliver—behind for good.

After she was finished packing, she slipped down to the ballroom to double check that everything was in place for gingerbread Paris to shine. Satisfied that nothing needed any last minute touch ups, she retreated to the quiet sanctuary of her room to prepare for the evening's festivities.

Posie had only brought one dress in anticipation of needing something nice to wear at the final event. A deep green silk dress that complimented her vibrant red hair and went perfectly with the necklace Oliver had made for her. The delicate clock pendant, shaped like a miniature horse, hung elegantly around her neck. As she looked at herself in the mirror, a pang of sorrow gripped her heart. The beautiful trinket was a tangible reminder of Oliver and the time they had spent together.

Sighing, she chided herself. "The whole reason you came to Long Point was for the job. Don't forget."

Tucking her cell phone and lipstick into a small clutch with a dainty gold chain for a strap, she was ready for the evening. Up to this point she had been so busy she had completely forgotten to get a good picture of gingerbread Paris. She would have to get one at the party.

When she joined the party it was already in full swing. Men in tuxedos and women in shimmering dresses moved through the magnificent ballroom. Every element had come together under Georgina's instructions; the twinkling lights, the fragrant pine, and the melodies of classical Christmas tunes filled the air.

Gingerbread Paris stood as a centerpiece against one long wall now full of food. A testament to her creativity and hard work, it drew admiration from every guest who came near.

Posie remained in a state of limbo, afloat between joy and grief. The anticipation of seeing Oliver, the anticipation of leaving him forever, all of it seemed surreal as she accepted compliments in a daze.

Georgina, radiant with joy, approached Posie with a wide smile. " Posie, you've outdone yourself! It's magnificent, truly magnificent!" She exclaimed, genuinely thrilled with the result. "You've made this party unforgettable."

Posie felt a swell of pride, grateful all of her efforts had not gone unnoticed. "Thank you, Georgina."

Georgina placed a hand heavy with diamond rings on Posie's arm. "Did you get your extra check? You did such a remarkable job I wanted to give you a bonus, but R.C. said if I gave it as a Christmas gift you could avoid paying taxes." She laughed at her husband's cleverness.

"I did, thank you so much."

"My favorite is the carousel and the music! It's delightful."

"Yes, that was Oliver's idea." Posie ventured the question. "Have you seen him yet?"

Georgina dismissed the question with a wave. "Oh, he never comes to these things. He's such a recluse." Posie tried to hide the shadow that fell over her face, but nothing escaped Georgina Andreanakis when she wanted to pay attention. With sympathy in her eyes, she said, "I know you two have grown…fond of each other. And, do you know what? When I realized yesterday that Cleo isn't interested in him romantically, I thought, why not Posie?" She leaned in closer. "But dear, he is a little bit of an odd duck. I'm not sure he'll ever be, well, *strong* enough for a romantic relationship."

Her words were a bittersweet pill to swallow. On one hand, she had basically given her blessing to the relationship. But on the other hand, she had spoken Posie's biggest fear out loud.

Cleo joined them, allowing Posie to change the subject. "You look beautiful tonight, Cleo."

Cleo enjoyed the compliment without blushing, a sign of

confidence Posie attributed to her blossoming romance with Finn. She gestured to Posie's dress, her eyes landing momentarily on her necklace, before answering, "You, too! I've never seen you out of your chef clothes."

"Neither of you are cooking tonight. You've earned some time off. Make sure to have some champagne!" Georgina told them.

Resigned to the possibility that she would not see Oliver at all, Posie turned from gingerbread Paris to find the nearest waiter with a tray of champagne. Perhaps she could drown her misery in bubbles.

That's when her gaze fell on him. Standing by the Christmas tree, looking at her. The very spot where he had given her the necklace. The same quiet glow of happy hope in his eyes. The same slow smile. Although, this time, he was in a tuxedo and looked every inch the gallant heir to Long Point.

Posie's heart fluttered madly in her chest. She couldn't catch her breath. He moved toward her, ignoring every other human being in the room, keeping his eyes locked to hers.

When he reached her he made a half bow, only letting his eyes leave hers to take in her dress and necklace before extending his hand. "May I have this dance?"

Speechless, she accepted, and within moments they were gliding across the dance floor while the orchestra played an elaborate and lively rendition of Jingle Bells.

"I think this might be our song," Oliver laughed, smiling down at her.

Posie didn't know whether to laugh or cry. So she danced. With Oliver guiding her every step, the people and the lights swept by, she only had eyes for him.

Between the music and the dancing there was no time to speak, but they didn't need words. They only needed each other, she could feel that truth in her bones. As long as the dance lasted they could remain lost in each other and forget about the rest of the world.

They finished Jingle Bells and two more songs. When they were going for number four with God Rest Ye Merry Gentlemen, another couple on the dance floor twirled a little too close behind Oliver and bumped him as they passed. He pulled Posie into him stiffly, protectively, even as all of the color drained from his face. For the first time since they had begun to dance, his eyes left hers and took in the crowded dance floor.

"Are you all right?" she asked, aware that there were more people surrounding them than when Jingle Bells had been playing.

"Yes," he nodded curtly. He still wouldn't look at her.

She didn't believe he was okay, and could tell he was deter-mined to keep dancing even if the other people were making him uncomfortable. "I'm a little thirsty, would you like to stop and get a drink?"

Oliver's eyes shot back to hers. "Of course."

He immediately led her off the dance floor straight back to gingerbread Paris. Too late they both realized Grandfather Reynolds had materialized in front of the Eiffel tower while they were mesmerized with each other on the dance floor. He was having a loud conversation with another distinguished gentleman Posie recognized as one of the posse who had come upon her and Oliver kissing.

In true form, Grandfather Reynolds was poised to make a loud disparaging remark and they had arrived just in time to overhear him.

"What use this, Ellison? It's all nonsense and a waste of money. Take this ridiculous monstrosity. A city made of gingerbread."

"It's Paris," Ellison interjected.

"Whatever it is, it isn't worth what we spent on it, that's for certain."

Posie would have walked away, removed herself from the old man's presence, but he happened to turn suddenly and she found herself face-to-face with him. She couldn't leave and give him the satisfaction of running her off.

He looked at her coolly, distaste in his eyes.

"Good evening," Posie said, holding her back straight, willing herself not to do something stupid like curtsy.

Grandfather Reynolds narrowed his eyes then looked at Oliver standing next to her. He shook his head in disgust and pushed past them.

"Grandfather," Oliver said forcefully. Grandfather Reynolds stopped short and turned back. Oliver continued, "A little more respect would be appropriate, don't you think?"

"A little more respect?" Grandfather Reynolds asked slowly...sarcastically. "For the cookie baker?"

Oliver lost his composure. "What is your problem with gingerbread, Grandfather? Or is it Paris you don't like? Or maybe it's Christmas?" Grandfather Reynolds glared at his grandson's outburst, but Oliver kept on. "Yes, it's an elaborate dessert, but since when did this family have a problem with elaborate anything?" He gestured to every corner of the magnificent ballroom where guests were beginning to notice the heated conversation. "Have you seen where we live? Its a mansion, almost a castle. Why must you always belittle anything that has even a modicum of joy or the Christmas spirit?"

Grandfather Reynolds scoffed. "Christmas spirit doesn't pay the bills, Oliver." With a withering glance at Posie he continued, "Once again, you've lost focus on what matters most."

"And what is that, Grandfather? Business? Is that what matters?"

Grandfather Reynolds straightened to his full height, which was slightly taller than Oliver. "Family business," he stressed the word family heavily. "Sentimentality won't secure the future of Long Point, boy."

Oliver laughed, but there was no humor in it. "You may understand business, but I don't think you understand family at all."

Grandfather Reynolds' face tightened and his voice was icy. "Oliver, you're being blinded by this girl. She's only after our wealth."

The accusation stung. Insult and injury boiled in Posie's chest, but before she could say anything, Oliver was toe-to-toe with his grandfather. "We had a deal," he said quietly between his teeth.

Grandfather waved dismissively, but he looked taken aback at his grandson's intensity. People were staring, pausing in their merry making at the scene unfolding in front of gingerbread Paris.

Mr. Ellison stepped in to defuse the situation with a light hearted smile. He put his hand on Grandfather Reynolds' back. "Truth be told, old boy, it was my wife that convinced me to sign those contracts." He nodded in Posie's direction. "After she spent the day decorating cookies with Georgina and the others."

Flustered at this announcement, Grandfather Reynolds pulled away from Oliver, grumbling something Posie couldn't quite make out. She didn't care to try and figure it out either. What she did care about was Oliver, and he wasn't doing very well.

He seemed to have noticed the crowd of people standing and watching the heated argument for the first time. His face was white, his features tight. His breath came fast and shallow. Posie understood immediately that he was near a panic attack, if not already experiencing one.

Cornered, with nowhere to turn, he gave one last look at Posie and took off, escaping the people, the party, and his grandfather.

CHAPTER 21

Ignoring the curious glances directed at her, Posie weaved through the lively, crowded ballroom. She had to see Oliver and knew exactly where to find him. The heat of the room felt oppressive, as if Long Point was determined to keep her trapped at the Christmas Party while Oliver was suffering.

Posie set her jaw and pressed on. She could be determined, too.

Cleo appeared beside her. "Are you okay?"

Fidgeting with the horse pendant on her necklace, Posie nodded, but struggled to contain her emotions. "I...I need to leave. I have to go see Oliver."

Understanding the urgency, Cleo offered her support. "I know a shortcut out of here."

Soon they were ducking into the servant's hall through the secret door set into the side of one of the ballroom enclaves. The very same door she and Oliver had climbed out of when they had been hiding from his Grandfather days ago. Those days seemed like months to Posie. So much had gone on between them since then. So much more needed to be said.

"Are you sure you don't want me to come with you?" Cleo asked.

She had brought Posie quickly through the servant's halls to the back door servant entrance and found her a heavy coat, hat and boots to wear into the freezing night.

But Posie had insisted she go to the carriage house alone.

"I'll be all right. I don't want you to miss the party." She smiled bravely.

Cleo smiled back. "I hope you two work everything out."

Posie gave her new friend a quick hug and struck out on her own across the winter garden, mute with snow.

The air grew colder the farther she went, leaving behind the warmth of the celebration. Snowflakes danced in the night air, and the distant sounds of the party faded into the serene stillness of the estate.

Her feet took her quickly, if somewhat awkwardly in borrowed boots, along the path that led to Oliver's house. Her breath formed misty clouds. Her heart ached to see him, comfort him, thank him for standing up against his formidable grandfather on her behalf.

The ache only expanded when Oliver opened the front door. Still in his tuxedo, but without the jacket, he had already loosened the bow tie and unbuttoned several of the top buttons of his shirt.

Holding a crystal glass of scotch in one hand, he looked at her with distant surprise, as if they were far away from each other and he could barely make out who she was from his vantage point.

"Posie..."

"Oliver...I..." The feelings swarming through her soul would not translate into words. All she wanted to say remained trapped inside, rushing through every cell in her body with no chance of release.

They held perfectly still, looking at each other. Oliver strangely removed. Posie feeling more and more like a lost little girl. Even the heavy coat and hat she wore, which were several sizes too big, seemed symbolic of how she didn't quite fit in.

Without a word, Oliver turned and retreated into the living room, leaving the door open as an invitation. Yet, not a very warm one.

The carriage house was dark. Not even the Christmas lights had been turned on. Posie did not remove her coat or hat, even though the temperature inside was warm enough. Something told her there was still a chill to be warded off.

When she entered the living room she found Oliver slumped into the corner reading chair, balancing his scotch on its arm.

"Oliver," she spoke gently, her voice breaking the silence. He turned, his eyes reflecting the storm within. "Are you okay?"

A few moments passed as he absorbed her question then he gave her a wry smirk. "No, I don't think I'm okay. I don't think I'll ever be okay." He took a gulp of scotch.

When she had made her way through the icy night to the carriage house, Posie had been wrapped up in her own feelings. She hadn't considered that Oliver wouldn't receive her with open arms. The man she had come to know, considerate and kind with a keen mind and quick sense of humor, seemed to be eroding right in front of her eyes. Caustic self-criticism had taken him over.

She searched for a way to break through to him. "I wanted to thank you."

He furrowed his brow. "Thank me?"

"For standing up to your grandfather."

"Oh, that," he snorted a derisive laugh. "That went over like a lead balloon didn't it? I'm sure it didn't change his mind. I'm sure it didn't change a single atom in even one of his stubborn old brain cells."

"I thought it was very brave of you."

Avoiding the compliment, he looked away from her, but she could still see raw emotion in his eyes. "If I was brave, Posie—truly brave—I would have told him off years ago and left this place."

His words squeezed her heart so much it hurt, but she didn't know how to help.

"The deal with your grandfather," she prompted gently, "what was it about?"

Oliver shot her a meaningful look, aiming to shield her pride, not his own. He leaned forward in the chair, resting his elbows on his knees before locking eyes with her. "I told him I would re-dedicate myself to business, to all of our family interests. I would take it more seriously and do what he wanted if he...if he would lay off of you. Stop insinuating you were after my money. Just leave you alone."

Posie caught her breath. She touched her throat with her fingertips. Surprised to have been the subject of such a conversation and agreement between Oliver and his imposing grandfather.

Oliver dropped his gaze to the floor and muttered, "A lot of good that did in the end."

Posie laughed, a self-conscious sound that brought them both back to the moment.

Oliver put his scotch down on the coffee table and fixed his eyes on hers. His expression shifted, remorse coloring his features. "I'm sorry about making a scene at the party."

"You don't have to apologize. It didn't bother me. I told you, I thought you were brave."

He smirked, but this time there was no bitterness in it. Letting his eyes wander all the way down her body then back up, he took in her makeshift outerwear, her green silk dress underneath, and the gleam of the golden horse pendant necklace at her neck.

"Do you know how beautiful you are?" he asked softly.

A warm tingle spread from the top of her head to the tips of her toes. There he was. Her Oliver had returned.

A raucous jangle of sounds erupted from her clutch purse hidden deep in the folds of the heavy coat. Her cell phone was ringing.

Oliver scowled, the technology always an irritation to him. Especially in this moment.

"Sorry, hang on." Posie managed to get the phone out of her purse before the fourth ring and answered it. "Hello?"

"Miss Posie, it's Thomas." The chauffeur's deep voice a sudden reminder that her time was up. "I'm in front of the carriage house. I have your luggage. The roads are pretty icy tonight. If you want to make your train, we need to leave now."

She pinched the bridge of her nose, wishing she hadn't been so eager to make her exit from Long Point when she bought her train ticket. "Yes, okay. I'll be right out."

His turn to be silent, Oliver watched her hang up and tuck the phone away.

"I have to go," she said. To her surprise, he didn't object.

Oliver nodded, a silent acknowledgment of the inevitable. His voice caught in his throat when he responded, "Of course. You're going home."

"Yes, home...my bakery...my real life."

Pain flinched in Oliver's eyes, but he managed to cover it up quickly with a warm smile. "Right, it's time you returned to your real life."

His words followed her as the car whisked her away from

Long Point, and haunted her on the lonely train ride all the way back to New York.

CHAPTER 22

Posie wasn't sure which was worse, being the only person sitting alone on the train on Christmas night and watching all of the loving couples and families who were traveling together, or stepping into her dormant bakery before the sun rose the next morning. Very different surroundings, yet the feeling was the same.

Numb, but with a dull ache in the center of her body, interrupted occasionally by a nearly unbearable pang of grief.

Both situations were awful. She felt awful. Everything was awful.

Even two generous checks to deposit into her bank later that day and the satisfaction of completing a job well done couldn't lift her mood. The whole world seemed cold, grey, and joyless as she brushed a light dusting of snow off of her jacket and shuffled into the bakery kitchen to prepare for the morning.

Without her assistants, who weren't scheduled to return from their Christmas breaks until the next day, she set about the tasks of baking some croissants, both the plain and chocolate variety, by herself. She also made several dozen extra large muffins, blueberry, banana nut, and chocolate chip. And, lastly, one of her favorite morning selections, scones. She made cranberry orange, lavender lemon, and vanilla bean scones to round out the selection.

It seemed like ages since she had created such small and simple treats and she let herself get lost in the process. Knowing the recipes by heart and using all of her specialty equipment made the work go by quickly. Soon the little corner bakery filled with the comforting scents of fresh baked goods.

"And no royal icing in sight," she said ruefully.

Flicking the Open sign on, she unlocked the door. There was no reason to expect a huge rush of customers. They rarely saw anything close to a rush of customers at her little out of the way place and it was early on a quiet morning, but she was ready to welcome a few at least.

Technically, with Georgina's generous bonus, she had enough money she could stop serving the public and try to only book high end cake clients, but she didn't want to do that just yet. With the mood she was in, it was probably best to invite people into her world instead of pushing them away, even if they were just customers. A bakery filled with people enjoying a cup of coffee and a scone might be soothing and make her feel less alone.

"Coffee!" she exclaimed, realizing she hadn't made any yet.

The bell on the bakery door jingled as Posie was busy setting up the coffee bar.

With her back to the door, she called over her shoulder, "Good morning, I'll be right with you."

When there was no answer, she turned to see who had come in.

"Surprise!" Bella exclaimed, raising her arms up and out dramatically.

Mason stood right behind her carrying a gift basket, his

height allowing him to beam at Posie over the top of Bella's head. He raised the basket up for her to see. "Merry Christmas, we brought cheese and wine!"

"Well, it's a belated Merry Christmas. But we're still on holiday time, right?" Bella asked, greeting Posie with a big hug. She held her at arm's length. "You've grown, haven't you?"

Posie brushed aside the silly comment. "I've only been gone a week."

"I don't know, my Mom used to say I'd grown after I got home from visiting my grandparents over the weekend," Mason said.

Posie had to laugh. "Mason, you're still growing, aren't you?"

He pointed at her. "Touché."

"Posie! We missed you so much!" Bella grinned, happy to have her friend back.

"I missed you guys, too. How did your annual Christmas party go?"

"So busy, but very well in the end." Bella answered while she led Posie to the nearest window table. "But I want to hear about your holiday. Did Paris turn out?"

Posie nodded and smiled a little too brightly, hoping to keep her heartbreak to herself for at least a little while longer. She didn't feel up to explaining everything that had happened at Long Point with Oliver just now. "It turned out very well. Do you guys want some coffee or a scone?"

"I'll get it," Mason volunteered.

Posie had no choice but to sit across from Bella and answer her questions. Of which, her friend had many.

"I bet it was gorgeous. Did you take pictures? I'd love to see it!"

"I didn't get any pictures."

"What?! Why didn't you take pictures?" Bella was surprised and disappointed.

Mason brought three cups of coffee and three cranberry orange scones to the table and sat down next to Bella.

"I don't know, it was very busy, lots to do. I just forgot."

"Maybe they had a photographer there who'll send you one," Bella suggested.

Mason nudged Bella. "I think she's too worn out to worry about that."

Posie nodded and took a sip of coffee. She tried not to make a face. She had always thought her bakery served great coffee, but she'd been spoiled by Rafael's brew for a week.

She sighed. Was nothing ever going to be the same after Long Point? Was her whole world always going to pale in comparison? Emotion rose in her throat and she had to fight back tears as she stared disappointedly into her cup.

"What's that? Why are you sighing?" Bella studied Posie's face.

"What?"

"You sighed. Like, audibly sighed. What's the matter?"

Posie squirmed in her chair. "Nothing's the matter, I'm just tired. Tell her, Mason. Tell her I look tired."

Mason didn't answer. His attention had been drawn to something outside and down the street a ways. Whatever it was, he was watching it with confusion.

Bella nudged him. "Pay attention. I need you on my side or she'll never tell me what's bugging her." When Mason still didn't respond, Bella followed his gaze. "What are you looking at?"

Still distracted, he answered, "A horse...no, two horses."

Bella strained to see what he was seeing, but his superior height made it impossible. Impatient, she asked, "What, like a carriage ride?"

"No, it's one guy on a horse. Leading another horse without a rider."

Posie's hand froze where she had been lifting a scone to her mouth to take a bite.

"Haven't you ever seen a man riding a horse before?" Bella teased.

Mason shrugged, still watching. "Yeah, I don't know. This guy has a look about him. And it's quite a horse. Big and black."

Posie's heart raced in her chest. She placed her scone back on its plate and wiped her hands on a napkin. Her palms were sweaty and she was filled with desperate hope, but she didn't dare turn to look for herself.

"What's the horse without the rider look like?" she asked, trying to sound nonchalant.

Bella gave her a sharp look. "Why is everybody so worried about some random guy and his horse."

"Horses," Mason corrected her. "There are two. And to answer your question, Posie, the other one's a buckskin."

Posie's legs felt like jello. She wanted to stand up and rush outside to see for herself, but she didn't trust they would hold her up. Without thinking, her hand went to her neck and she took hold of her horse pendant.

Bella noticed and cocked her head to the side, giving Posie a curious look. "What is going on with you? Are you hyperventilating?"

Continuing with his play-by-play of what was coming down the sidewalk, Mason let out a surprised laugh. "Oh, man, and there's a dog with them. It's huge! I thought it was a bear for a second."

Leaving only the clatter of dishes and her stunned friends behind, Posie pushed away from the table and ran out into the snow. She stopped short in the middle of the sidewalk.

Her heart pounding so hard she thought it might jump out of her chest.

There he was.

Oliver.

Riding Neptune and leading Honeycomb. Looking as out of place and uncomfortable as a man could look. Drawing attention from everybody on the street. Keeping his eyes trained intently on the front of her bakery and, when she came out, on her and her alone.

Oliver had come for her.

She smiled and waved then put her hands to her mouth, afraid she would cry. He held up one hand and waved back briefly, his own smile full of both hope and uncertainty.

Hagrid reached her before Oliver did. Barking and circling her with such excitement she had to laugh. "Hagrid, I've missed you!" The dog made such a ruckus she couldn't explain what was going on to Bella and Mason, who had stepped outside the bakery and were watching the scene with confused delight.

Oliver stopped Neptune when he reached her, but he didn't get down. He took a couple of deep breaths like he had just climbed a hill and looked at her with adoration.

"What are you doing here?" Posie asked, wonder in her voice.

"Oh, right, well, actually I was hoping your establishment carried gingerbread cookies. We seem to have run out of gingerbread and I...well, Hagrid, had a real hankering for some."

Posie chuckled and stepped forward to stroke Honeycomb's soft nose. "Hagrid doesn't like gingerbread. So I know you're making that up."

Wrinkling his brow, Oliver pretended to be flustered at being found out in a lie. Though she suspected his nervousness was real, he was still trying to make her laugh.

"Okay, you caught me. I made that up. The real reason, the actual honest to goodness reason we came is..." He pulled his riding coat open to reveal a medium sized box he had been balancing on the saddle in front of him. Bravely ignoring the small crowd of pedestrians who had slowed down around them to see what was going on, Oliver dropped deftly to the ground with the box in one hand and handed it to her. "You forgot this."

The box was green and the exact style of box that had held her necklace, but this box was bigger and heavier. She pulled the lid off and saw the horse and sleigh clock peeking out of a nest of green tissue paper.

"The clock! I thought you were just lending it to me." She smiled, charmed by the gift and by his presence.

"Yes, well, it's a set you see. The clock and the necklace." He cleared his throat. "They, um, well, they were made to go together."

"I see." She gave him a teasing smile. "You brought Neptune and Honeycomb all the way into the city to bring me this clock?"

He laughed, his eyes bright, the slightest flirtation in his smile. "All right, all right, the truth." He sighed heavily as if he was about to make a confession. "The truth is I wanted to go for a ride." He paused and his eyes searched hers with an earnestness she felt to her core. "But I didn't want to go without you."

Tears filled Posie's eyes. Her throat tightened. "I thought you couldn't leave Long Point."

"Oh no, you see, that's a little off from what I said. I said I was *afraid* to leave Long Point."

She sniffed, her eyes wet. "And you're not afraid anymore?"

He let out an embarrassed laugh and looked at the ground, then glanced quickly at Bella and Mason, and the pedestrians watching them, before looking back at her. "I'm terrified." He grew more serious, his voice cracking when he said, "But I realized last night, after you left, that more than anything else I was afraid of never seeing you again."

Posie couldn't hold back her tears any longer. Several rolled down her cheeks. Oliver reached up and wiped them away. His hands trembled as they touched her skin, sending shivers down her spine.

He leaned closer to her, almost whispering, "The truth is, Posie, you've captured me. You've taken hold of my heart. Of my soul. And I don't think I can ever feel right again unless you are by my side."

"Oh, Oliver," she whispered back, but that was where her words ended and the tears took over.

He held her face with both hands, touching his forehead to hers, creating a quiet, intimate place for them alone in the middle of the New York City sidewalk. "We don't have to stay at Long Point, either. We can go anywhere you like. We can even stay here..." He closed his eyes and took a deep breath. "With all of these...people...if need be."

Posie's tears of joy turned to laughter and she wrapped her arms around Oliver's neck. "Don't look at anyone else. Only look at me."

He pulled away and gave her a quizzical smile. "Only you?"

"Only me."

Grinning, he slipped his hands around her waist. "I can do that."

"Good...and Oliver?"

"Yes, Posie?"

"Shut up and kiss me."

He did.

Once again, Neptune and Honeycomb stood by, like

sentries guarding them from the prying eyes of interested bystanders.

Posie lost herself in the warm embrace of the man she loved and in what sounded like a land faraway, Hagrid barked happily, nearby pedestrians applauded, Mason called out a happy shout of encouragement, and Bella exclaimed for all to hear, "I knew it wasn't all about cookies!"

The End

ALSO BY DARCI BALOGH

<u>Sugar Plum Romance Series</u>

1. Charlotte's Christmas Charade

2. Bella's Christmas Blunder

3. Posie's Christmas Predicament

<u>Sweet Holiday Romance Series (Box Set - great value!)</u>

Feel-good romances to get you in the spirit for Halloween, Thanksgiving, Christmas and a brand New Year!

1. Enchanting Eve

2. Love is at the Table

3. Mistletoe Madness

4. New Year in Paradise

<u>The Mighty Aphrodite Writing Society</u>

1. Beach Retreat at Turtle Cove

2. Beach Wedding at Turtle Cove

<u>Dream Come True Series</u>

Clean and wholesome women's romance fiction

1. Her Scottish Keep

2. Her British Bard

3. Her Sheltered Cove

<u>Lady Billionaire Series</u>

Clean and wholesome women's romance fiction

1. Ms. Money Bags

2. Ms. Perfect

<u>Love & Marriage Series</u>

Steamy, emotional, relatable characters, these older woman, younger man women's fiction stories are both racy and romantic.

1. Stars in the Sand

2. For Love & For Money

3. The Quiet of Spring

ABOUT THE AUTHOR

Darci Balogh is an author and filmmaker who spent much of her life living both in and near the majestic Rocky Mountains of Colorado.

She now resides in the beautiful state of Michigan near Lake Huron. She has two amazing grown daughters, too many dogs, and an aversion to dusting.

Her fiction is a blend of women's fiction and romance (both sweet and spicy) with strong female characters and charming leading men. She has been a writer since she was a child and enjoys crafting stories into novels and screenplays.

Big surprise, some of her favorite pastimes are reading and watching movies. Classic British TV is high on her 'Like' list, along with quietly depressing detective series all while sipping coffee with heavy cream.